ANSFORM

☛Elucidativo. Contundente – este ANIZAR de Louis Armand – um possível mergulho no Alentejo Profundo, anotado aqui e ali por barrascos pontuais, saudosismos d'algibeira ou compadrio. Álibis entre autarcas, gigolos e chaparros – tudo a coberto de moléstia salazarenta. **Rui Baião**

☛This dark, humorous tall tale sparkles with wicked & hallucinatory power. A surreal exploration of existence & perception unfolds amidst the backdrop of an alternative version of Portuguese history. As the narrative navigates through disjointed scenes & introspective musings, every twist & turn revealing new layers of speculation & mystery, the protagonist, Albufarkas, undertaker maudit & artiste manqué, is a curious anomaly, a relic of a future that has already happened, "a refugee from the fate evolution had in store". Somewhere between James Joyce's *Ulysses* & Thomas Pynchon's best work, ANIZAR shows Louis Armand once again writing dangerously about the fractured psyche & corroded self. **Michel Delville**

☛Hyper-imaginative & wildly comico-critical glossolaliac streams are spurted by a mocking sceptic called Albufarkas. His alter-ego Antifarkus "knows he's mad," but does "the world"? His writings, he says, "shld be excessively made, so even the dimmest of dimwits catches on: understatements, my dears, are for the undertaken." Louis Armand's tangled enigma is full of parody, nonsensical monologue, &, as if from dreams on the edge of nightmare, carnivalesque vulgar & ultra tricky characters. This gripping seductive mystery is located in a Portuguese municipality that has no renowned author for tourists to consume. Tourists – *Pare de sofrer, existe uma solução!* Stop suffering, there is a solution! – read this startling work, ANIZAR. **Pam Brown**

☛A multiple & playful narrative, ANIZAR presents itself as a theatre scene but it cannot be characterized as theatre. Its title is the name of its location, but this name does not mean anything. The name of one of its important characters, Albufarkas, is like dead letters, in other words, like the sign of a lost anteriority or any present. These paradoxes identify writing to nothingness, but make it a vital exercise & open to many free imaginings, literary archeologies & fanciful or concrete realities, & narrative & existential orientations & disorientations. The title in Portuguese that introduces the last lines of ANIZAR designates an ultimate disorientation: "Medo in la madugrada" / "Fear in the morning," & the literal end of its fiction: the man whose name is dead letters is found... dead. ANIZAR is at once a vital exercise & an enjoyable practice of literary deconstruction, reflexivity & irony. **Jean Bessière**

AN
IZ
AR

ANZAR · 1
ANIZAR · T

☛In the glitchy Portuguese town of Anizar, Armand introduces the reader to an eccentric cast of characters. Armand's poetic prose shifts swiftly between Albufarkus' comic dialogues with his alter-ego; musings of the poet João Sobremango; witty exchanges between theatre manager Carbonara Inverso & librarian-dominatrix, Senhora Epimedia; & the mysterious murder of Caesar Salazarini. In ANIZAR Armand has adapted his constantly erupting, playful writing into a fast-paced, delightfully comic novella." **DJ Huppatz**

☛Most literature represents a latent fascism. The edifice of meaning is a living death. Thus there is a certain crime against the corporate mafia & the police state that can only assume the form of a simple poetic act. And it is always your own self staring back at you, an event for which there can be no recorded image…. The pages are a repository of used time, corrosive anecdotes dredged up from a fast-decaying memory, a state of evolving disrepair, reified unmeaning — relentless episodic soliloquy & dialogue, a mind in disregard with itself, a mind in the process of unhinging: glimpses of mutant academia, Salazar's ghosts, Madame Blavatsky channelling the everyday: fatal ectopic pregnancy, Mars ascendant, Roma ultras beating the crap out of a mouldy, braille-eared vampyr. It's said that all the voices heardwithin the context of the story can be heard by the characters themselves.

Ostensibly, a portrait of the Portuguese municipality of Beja, painted in runic cryptomorphs (two objects that are equivalent, but not obviously equivalent). It means nothing, it could mean everything — our mortal coil in crosshairs stencilled red, where death is the most common way of life — non-existence, an indeterminate being-here, where alienation is love's counterpart…. Beja: a nomadic people living between the Nile & the Red Sea. (Coincidence?) And so we are propelled from the particular to the universal, the archetypal, before being flung back into that eternal pilgrimage to a home that was never there in the first place.

Yes, a character is writing something, the very book we are reading, an autobiographic novel minus plot — blue ink stain on fingertips, watching the entropy escalate…. Because there is actually no body, there never was a body. A vision emerges from neanderthal high sierra, traces of Rimbaud gunrunning in Ethiopia, Lowry under a volcano, Guyotat ejaculating in the Algerian desert. . . . The soundtrack is unquestionably Morricone, as each scene drifts through a delirious exile: someone does not want the history to end — requiem for a destiny, prehistoric rain…. The only available suspect is time itself.

Here is a novel that seeks deliverance in abortion of the self, through a vulva-like talisman — one in the eye of the needless. Einstein got it wrong: gravity is a disease. Everyone needs an alibi. **Richard Makin**

ISBN 978-1-7394310-3-7

Equus Press
Birkbeck College, 43 Gorden Square,
London WC1 H0PD, United Kingdom

typeset by Lazarus
cover design by Interior Ministry

The author wishes to thank Mariana Gomes, Emanuel Cameira, Rui Baião, Joshua Cohen, Lena Inverno, Mark Divo, Sónia Calvário, Leopoldina Almeida, João Guerreiro, Cristina Matos, João Espinho, Nádia Mira, Vitor Domingos, Deolinda Tavares, Patrícia Santos & – as ever – David Vichnar, for making this book possible.

ANIZAR
LOUIS ARMAND

EM BOCA FECHADA
NÃO ENTRA MOSCA

A receding wall of heat & the plain, neither for the first nor last time, conjugates a reprieved psyche from sheer expanse of terrain, baleful yet serene as the stupefied juggernaut, one pale eye soldered in place, the other a red orb of liquid glass drooling down into barometric haze the dizzying birds wheel upon.

Here we set our stage. A proscenium, horizon-wide, flung open to dusk's amphitheatrics. The cubist array of streets, whitewash & terracotta, obsolete TV aerials, flickering lights, voices & birdspeak & thrumming of an orchestra tuning up. Venus, first among primadonnas, makes her entrée. A hot wind blusters into applause. What audience we might conjure is left wiping dust from their eyes for the entire first act, so it's only the second that counts. Our primadonna might just as well pick her nose while dwarfs tumble around the stage, or vice versa, but can it be called art if no-one else sees it?

History, too, may be a dream, but we are not the dreamer. Nor is this some Cartesian theatre of the mind but, so to speak, life in the round, a real flesh & blood production under rafters, treading the boards, exiting by the wings or straight into the orchestra pit (w/ a bona fide orchestra, Eli Põe conducting; Meyer Gordo, the "stringsection detective," on 1st violin). Houselights dim, curtain rises, the scene opens: a wall w/ crumbling stucco, a faded blue metal door, & beside the door a torn poster flapping in the wind. The letters ANIZAR legible in bold print. It means nothing. It cld mean anything. And so we are propelled from the particular to the universal. ANIZAR. Taken as a sign, a signal, a subliminal semaphore, for an egregious geographeme, orphaned, expropriated, incompletely exxed-out by vying contretemps, unpronounceable consonants, contractions & cataracts natural & unnatural, cardinal points & cartographical approximations, or just something that once bungled out of the mouth of some pre-eminent pagan, sampling the view from a cave above a freshwater fountain, a speech-sign drawn on the rock, a chanting stone, a songline, recounting how from this place the first apemen surveyed a flat Earth for many miles, gazing out at bison herds sweeping over the great alluvial sweep of the Baixo Alentejo from high sierra westward to the sea. ANIZAR! They, too, had their nomenclatures. ANIZAR! They, too, summoned the genii loci to become their genii hominis. ANIZAR! And did those hairy spirits know then who they served? Or who wld usurp them? How many moons since they fled, dissolved into the cracked clay like prehistoric rain?

Here, this non-word seems to say, once dwelt gods where now dwells the sole specimen of a missing link, all but forgotten because barely known & in any case unlikely ever to be missed. If theatre speaks in archetypes, then as the wind flaps the torn poster & the blue metal door creaks open on rusted hinges, so shall we behold our protagonist: Albufarkas, last of a long line of deadletters that turn up after the postal system's been abolished, like a residual organ that serves no purpose yet makes a show of functioning nonetheless, like a winning lottery ticket you find slipped between the pages of a book 20 years too late – in short, a perverse superfluity, what humxnity might've become had it lost the art of seeing itself reflected in everything. Is Albufarkas merely a refugee from the fate evolution had in store? The lemming who paused to take in the view? The inheritor of an acquired characteristic, perpetually at odds? A glitch in the grisaille transmitted from some lost subcircuit & slowly invading the entire picture? The Cartesian mind's submind come home to roost? (If a point deserves to be made at all, it shld be excessively made, so even the dimmest of dimwits catches on: understatements, my dears, are for the undertaken.)

The orchestra tenses, the backdrop parts where the now-open blue metal door leads through dark interstices to a room & a man inside that room. Take a moment for yr eyes to adjust. The man is hunched over a small table, barely wider than he is. For the time being, imagine that he's in the process of writing something. If you need to know what, pretend he's writing this. The room's the thing.

It's the kind of room you might expect to walk into in a novel without a plot, looking for a subtext to get you onto the next page. But that doesn't mean it will. The walls aren't any more lopsided than the walls in any other room in any other pre-literary setting. The plaster not more mottled, cracked, powdered, peeling or gaping onto portals of unfathomable masonry & rammed clay. The floors undulate rather than heave. The panelled ceiling isn't especially bowed & split. The scent of mildew & decay remains subtle or at least not sufficient to choke on. The dullness of the lamps not a complete obstacle to groping one's way. All in all, the room is of a species of nondescript, templated, marquee-tooled, overlaid w/ grunge straight out of the algorithm. As for the man in it? Take a look in the mirror, hahaha. What shld a vague commingling of expectation & disbelief look like? Picture someone sceptical of their own existence to such a degree they've resorted to poetry to disprove it. Ah! Exactly. Well you can't have it all yr own way, can you? Maybe it'd help if we let him recite some of the offending drivel? See, he sets aside his pen. Blue inkstains on fingertips. His mouth opens. The obscene & ruddy worm that inhabits it begins to writhe. He squints. A pair of thumbsmeared lenses creep down the bulbous nose. He coughs. A thin thread of spittle dangles from creased lower lip.

Voice. Loud. As if reading a telegram. All-caps.

TV NEWS REPORTS EXPERT SAYING WORLD LIKELY ADVANCED COMPUTER SIMULATION STOP.

Looks up. Ambiguous tone of voice. As if addressing an imaginary audience, colon.

You die & the image of something dies w/ you.

Bravo. (See if he can keep it up.)

Albufarkas takes a deep breath:

From now on just a settling of dust, the sifting of pixel-decay, slow data-rot, mildew on the motherboard, skeletons gradually unfleshed on the holodeck, a bad smell general across the array.

Pauses. Fixes his unsettling gaze upon the audience (that's you). Respires audibly. Attempts a smile of unfeigned sincerity:

Hello, looking even more yr radiant self today!

Fails. Goes on, determined to fail again better:

How wld it be, sitting out yr last days just watching the entropy accumulate, like the kind of phenomenal wealth it's impossible to spend? They haven't explained yet, a simulation of what? Evolution's battery-operated thumbscratcher? As for the others, hahaha. So this is where you wash up, at the end of the due-date? All the flotsam of Atlantis sunk under the sea, churned up again by tsunamis of dialectical history? The thought does cross one's mind: infernal. Frobenius cave-dwellers tuning the firelight to full-immersion cinema. Mr DeMille, we're ready for our closeup! Need never burn another celluloid reel to stay warm again, everything's already electron-minded, even death gets quantised, you wanna do the replay? Houston, we've got a prolegomenon! Picking up rumours about some kinda metaphysical realestate out there, been trying to mock up a sim ever since, see what we'd be getting ourselves into. Nothing like shooting blind to avoid taking a shot in the dark...

Long pause, catching his breath. Really, it's incredible he's gotten this far. A thesp in full unfettered flow. The weevils are popping out of the woodwork to take in the sight of it. Such loquacity! Right up there w/ "To pee or not to pee?" Just a teeny bit more, now. Come on, Albufarkas! Come on, boy!

Well as a species, you know, there are drawbacks any which way you look at it.

CASA DAS MÃOS

Albufarkas had written a letter to Imam Koan elaborating in microscopic detail his plans to resurrect the old ruin at number 10 rua Alferes Malheiro *w/ his own hands*, prompting the Imam to remark, "World is strange. For example, y're building a house w/ yr hands." Albufarkas considered the fivefingered khamsa of Fatimah, Innana, Ishtar, Tanit, the Kef Miryam, the Mano Pantea, settling finally for a trinket from a stall at the Roman Festival, a simple vulva-like talisman to ward off the Evil Eye. And hung it on a wall of the darkest room at the end of the house: the room w/ no windows. He called it, the room, for he was possessed at times by a poetic turn, the Golem's Sarcophagus. If evil resided anywhere on the premises, here he placed his bet. It was the kind of room a creature of dubious reality cld easily have expired in.

The house was 5 other rooms stacked up w/ a terrace on the roof. While every precinct of the house remained in a state of evolving disrepair, Albufarkas indulged in the creation of a Garden of Adonis, filling the terrace w/ potted earth. In due course these pots revealed a diverse abundance of plant-life. Tomatoes large & small, oranges, clementines, zucchinis ("black beauty"), artichokes, basil (multiple varieties), thyme, rosemary (2 varieties), lavender, red capsicum, jalapeños, pimientos de Padrón, a mango tree, guyaba, bougainvilleas (x2), to which later were added, on the balcony daubed in an unfortunate cast of blue, Agathe Scarlet (aka Agatha Christie Bloodbath), Solanum Jasminoides (aka Valerie Solanas) & a precocious hanging basket of purplewhite beachumbrella petunias. From the street, this *soi-disant* Casa das Mãos looked more like a melodrama in a cracked porcelain funerary urn juggled by mimes. Which in a sense it was.

Albufarkas had been called many things in his medium-long passage on this mortal coil, but not yet an undertaker, though he'd once, in his youth, & for some years, assiduously costumed himself as one, only to be mistaken for a poet instead. Which had pleased him up to a point &, in a lesser mortal, may easily have sown the seeds of his doom had he not in fact been doomed already, from birth, though not to (or even by) poetry. Presently, however, the new inhabitant of the House of Hands, w/ his flaring chin-beard & myopic occulars, his crystalgazer's djellaba (maroon&white striped) & curled babouches (bananaskin yellow), might've just as readily been taken for an Oedipalised TV soothsayer, w/ ratty straw widebrimmed sunhat (where jewelled turban wld've been customary) & Helvetian alpenstock. Ulcer-inducing in any props department. More to the point, this Albufarkas was the spitting image of one Monsieur Metastaise, confessed "bete noire," in postcard reproduction, circa 1907, snapped in the vicinity of the Biskra oasis, photographer unknown. The predilection for blue notwithstanding. For savage nudes in disconcerting repose. A postcard that cld be found, among several others (various, ostensibly unrelated), on the mantlepiece of the wide Alentejan fireplace that accounted for half of Albufarkas' kitchenette.

In matters of the spirit-world, Albufarkas considered himself strictly agnostic. To be the incarnation of the great dauber Metastaise, a mere caprice, haha, of coincidence fooling the eye. Unconsciously, y'd bet yr money on the mirror-opposite. The man was an artiste manqué. He even kept a drawer full of oil paints, that he'd caress in their tubes, run his fingers through pristine sable, sniff the linseed w/ the same longing as men of literature have been known to sniff their heroine's gusset. No fear, you may well say: he suffered prose like torture.

This hill, gawped Albufarkas – hand out-sweeping, weary eye tilted at the flat expanse, ocean-wise, from atop the mossy lichen-carpeted terraço (Caloplaca thallincola) – is the middenheap, the ancient accumulated compost, through which all of adjacent history & protohistory ferments & percolates, as from some noxious sibylline grot, into this unholy sludge of our gainsaid present epoch. (He leaned over the low wall & ogled briefly the precipice.) We live – oh we say we live, but heaven help us! – in a tide of vexatious effluent. But not only humxn destiny will be written by the fluid dynamics of such hideous substances. (He swung about, affecting a kind of flourish inside his djellaba. Apparently Albufarkas was naked underneath.) Once upon a time alchemists thought they cld bottle it, like Coca-Cola, pure gold. I mean, who'd've bet that one day half the planet wld pay to swill toiletcleaner? But it's not the same thing, no. We're *in* the toiletcleaner, *it's* drinking *us*!

Yawn! (his alterego, squinting & grimacing.) Up half the night watering the weeds. Man can't sleep on a gutload of piss. Nor history neither. Wars have been waged over lesser things. If you don't talk the lingo, yr average piss-artist doesn't stand a chance.

How many lingos, we'll never know. Dead. All dead. And no-one to mourn over them.

Time doth surely mime a most mysterious idiolect.

A goldfinch perched on the old TV aerial that stood high above the adjacent house. It scowled at Albufakas in annoyance. Shut up! it said. A swallow dashed past. Shut up! it said. A sparrow hopping across rooftiles said, Shut up! Swifts, magpies, pigeons, crows, all called out to Albufarkas to shut up. Oy-vey! Not one ounce of respect did the feathery creatures have for a man of his altitude, his leaning, his accoutrement! Albufarkas' alterego giggled. Shut up yrselves!

Well well well. Doolittle, I presume? Off w/ the birds, finally, eh, old coque? And you thought they enjoyed that dilapidated thesp routine y've been putting on every time you climb up here, prancing about w/ the Great Mind on display? Ah! Let guano rain! Let adulation nitrogenate the potted ferns!

What's serious is often disguised as its opposite: nature knows this intuitively. The jackdaw, for example. The hyena. The rat. The idiot.

Albufarkas' alterego stood there stroking his beard, chortling. In the raiment of his humour he paid Albufarkas no heed at all. Time washed over him while Albufarkas mutely genuflected, brooded, paced about & eventually departed, a man habituated to defeat. So much for dialogue. Once the strange antipyrine entered one of its Socratic trances, there was nothing Albufarkas or anyone else cld do. He traipsed down the corkscrew-stairs, down to the room at the end of the house & slumped there in the not-inclement gloom to doodle in his musebook. Plato to that hemlocked lunatic on the parapet. Well, perhaps if he cld system it, life wld make sense after all. At least the parts of it he was made to suffer. *He who does not write*, admonished his pen, *is free to run amok.*

But Antifarkas was the most unlike thing to amok & this caused Albufarkas no end of dismay. *Always what shld be obvious is a fool's errand.* He was afraid his words were more pompous even than usual. Time to turn over a new leaf. Or tear, tear them all out, & w/ scissors hack them up, or not bother about the scissors, hands wld do. Let the ruins fall where they may! Well he'd been down that road & try as he might the arrangements wldn't budge. Every word in its identical place time after time. Like calling heads on an uninterrupted streak. Return of the proverbial repressed, haha. As if the words, too, had entered into a trance. *Better to just write it down, all of it, the abortive action, the unrealised meaning, the realised unmeaning, no-one'll read it anyway.* Safe, yes, from scrutinising eyes. Or was it only Mind that scrutinised? How did he *know* those paperscraps tossed all over the floor always fell the same? Did the eyes commemorate the fact ad aeternam? Y'd need to write everything twice just to be sure! But then who was to say, some hidden hand, the moment yr attention slips, erasing & rearranging?

Meanwhile, up on the roof, sunset had melted the horizon. The constellations flickered on. A satellite streaked eastward across the sky. Albufarkas' ego-alterwise blinked. Oh Zion, where oh where is thy home of homes? He knew that Albufarkas was mad, but wld the world?

TEMPUS EDAX RECTUM

They venerated sword & ploughshare, carved in stone. Runic cryptomorphs. Nameless to their exhumers 3,000 years postfactum, like prima facie evidence of a crime w/ no identifiable corpse. A cracked pictogram for a murder weapon. The only available suspect, Time.

The terrace of the Museo Rainha D. Leanor commanded an uninterrupted view of the local kebab joint, Al-Moçonu.

Carbonara Inverso, sometime patroness, ex-diva of the Teatro Pax Julia, gazed down at the spectacle of Professor Fidelius stuffing his face w/ falafel & ketchup. What in god's name was he doing there when he was meant imminently to be speechifying at the Museum's Annual Meet-the-Peeps? They were handing out the prosecco now in plastic cups & very shortly must be ushered-in to the Rococo chapel, to be tortured on gnarly pews under the supplicating gazes of mutilated, boiled, disembowelled & crucified martyrs of Christendom. Listening to Fidelius prate through his beard for an hour about minor antiquities, under a fine spray of piquant spittle wld, by comparison...

Carbonara Inverso's companion leant his buttocks incautiously against the balustrade & surveyed the local intelligentsia milling about clutching free booze. His one astigmatic eye reminded her of Sartre. Which in turn reminded her that Simone de Beauvoir had lectured on the "woman question," on the very spot she, Carbonara Inverso, was presently standing, back in 1954, the year she, Carbonara Inverso, happened to've been conceived, in a rush of illconsidered inebriation between two first cousins of a once-respectable dynasty of olive-pluckers. Except she was never entirely sure which eye it was. Like the sun going round the Earth, or the Earth around the moon, depending on which way you looked at it, or them. They (herself & erstwhile companion Sobremango) had just managed to escape the company of Pontifax, who'd been slobbering about *The Penal Colony* ever since he'd returned from Mitteleuropa, to anyone afflicted enough to listen.

Sobremango (morosely, a lopsided squint):

People are such appalling creatures of alibi. They flee to Prague & beg forgiveness of Kafka. They flee to Buenos Aires & beg forgiveness of Borges. And when they flee to Lisbon, they beg forgiveness of Pessoa. Idiots, they've no idea of the danger they're exposing themselves to. They'd spare themselves & everyone else much regret by just throwing themselves off a bridge & getting it over w/. One look's all you need, to know none of them wld ever stand up, for even a minute, under interrogation.

And when they flee here, what do they pretend to beg forgiveness from?

No-one comes here.

Perhaps because there are no bridges. It isn't a fair contest.

At that moment the bow-wave of a long dry roll of thunder washed over them, coming from a sky empty of the slightest vapour. The culprit was long gone already.

Sobremango:

Teararsing up & down the peninsular in their hypersonic toys, when isn't there the whole Atlantic Ocean out there to piss about?

The war (Carbonara Inverso picked her teeth contemptuously) wld seem to be in the opposite direction.

There's always a war going on somewhere.

Not that y'd know it. (Carbonara Inverso pouted.) I'm not a doubter, it's just an observable fact.

From our present vantage, Sobremango opined, observable facts are relatively improbable. It wld be facile to picture a world w/out such distractions. Or if not a world, at least a well-endowed museum.

And yet I'd say the outlook is more universal, in temper if not in prospect.

This, here, or in general?

I can't generalise myself, I'm only able to be what I am.

Considered universally?

Yes.

So what are you, then, precisely?

Present & accounted for.

I feel the opposite. I've no faith in the present, nor to being accountable, simply by existing, "being here," even in yr exquisite company.

Irony will only get you so far.

Yes, yes, but once the clothes are off & y're engaged in congress, isn't that far enough? The rest takes care of itself, n'est-ce pas?

For that, one also requires self-deception.

Or another beverage? (Sobremango gestured w/ an empty plastic cup in the direction of the drinks table.) It comes w/ liabilities, however. Pontifax is standing guard over the bottles, we'll be lucky to get away a second time. He'll want to climb into bed w/ us.

Tedious as these occasions are, dearest, do try not to get ahead of yrself. It'll only end in embarrassment.

Life's too ridiculous to be embarrassed about anything.

Taking her cue, Senhora Epimedia, librarian & *sub rosa* dominatrix, materialised at Sobremango's elbow:

Maestro!

The distinction was pro forma, she gushed reflexively, playing to the TV cameras that hovered, like perpetual cherubim, at the back of her mind. Which, Sobremango postulated, was not so vast a distance, meaning she was the kind of woman habituated to being appreciated in close-up. Sobremango bent his head to take in the overall effect. It was a mistake. The librarian's cleavage reeked of patchouli & eczema. Faint bubbles of effervescence seemed to pop from the corners of Senhora Epimedia's mouth.

Our monthly book circle eagerly awaits yr next masterpiece!

When will you come to us, Maestro?

Her syllables frilled, follicled, fibulated, like endangered sea anemones. The undulations of her lips & tongue were indeed a kind of miracle to behold. It gave Sobremango the shivers. He saw his bones whitening on a coral reef, picked clean by the devourers. HERE LIES AHAB THE MONOMANIAC. Genius' last resting place, eh? Senhora Epimedia's beringed claw insinuated itself through the crook of Sobremango's left arm. Carbonara Inverso reached unceremoniously across & declawed:

Mine, darling.

It seemed she wanted him for herself, a little longer at least, till supply outstripped demand, possibly. Epimedia mooed for the cameras:

You must unprison the Maestro for the people! He is our national treasure!

Carbonara Inverso guffawed, she'd never heard anything so ridiculous in her life. Sobremango of the people! Viva Sobremango!

The crowd surged briefly & absorbed the librarian. They were once more, in a manner very much relative, alone. Carbonara Inverso gazed back over the parapet.

Ah! There was Fidelius wiping his mouth w/ a too inadequate paper napkin, edging up out of his seat, gathering suitjacket, briefcase & panama, crumbs of falafel freely distributed upon each. It seemed they'd have the lecture on time after all, within the accepted standard deviation. The Museum's guestlist had been well-lubricated, which was half the job done. The terrace swayed under the display of sweaty calico, a panoply of white on beige on rubicund. At least no-one was puking over the gargoyles.

The Maestro must give the introduction, said Carbonara Inverso w/ professional aplomb, causing the Red Sea to part.

Well so much for that, Sobremango shifted his buttocks off the balustrade & straightened his trouser-crease. He grimaced apologetically at the doomed Egyptians w/ their faces contorted in wonderment, expectation, annoyance. Groped for his notes. Frowned. Nodded, etc. A moment later he was being frogmarched through the doors. Pontifax blustered something auto-obsessed as they passed. Safe, then, for the time being. Though what was to follow, well, that was another matter entirely. What no-one else knew was that a special part of Sobremango's brain had been designed precisely for occasions such as these, where all he had to do was press play & let the tape run, then wait for the applause at the end, or better not to wait, better always to be on yr way somewhere, a man on the move, exeunt behind an arras, let the roses fall in yr wake, but under no circumstances look back, haha. Yes, well, archaeology, hahaha. Oh how perfectly he was in his element, like potassium, hahahaha.

Sobremango must've nodded off during the rest of the preambles, because the amphitheatre was suddenly a ruined temple afloat in a paradox of grey schist & copious bougainvillea. A voice a lot like his own was narrating the "scene":

Gaps in the bougainvillea, paintings w/ their backs turned, blank, the crumbling stucco portends, the revealed soul within, limewashed in guilty haste, always the neglected comes back in spasms, time never as present as it becomes, in rammed earth dissolved to talc, you prick it & out sift the emaciated years, trickling into a deluge nothing can scaffold, but a furnace sun that renders fugitive silicates to glass, gnarled windows where all the old illusions swim again, riverine in latent vermilion & white, *every inexplicable necessity contains a murder.*

With his eyes, Sobremango tries to paint out the shadows, smooth the inkstains into a background continuum. Blinks. Ah, but w/ the right eye nothing, almost nothing, you cld hold them apart at separate removes, just to get the world to resolve, bad enough w/ the head in two places, these constant trigonometries to take bearing, maintain, while up there, in the sky of mind, the swifts & swallows, drunk on parabolas, hyperbolas, the air a many-proportioned thing, woven in knots, cld time be also as we in our plurality traverse it, as it traverses us?

Or see in a flash all the joined filaments, drawing a line, the thread of it, Ariadne-like, in a Minotaur-maze, of void & formlessness, our mortal end in crosshairs stencilled red, a beast to be slain in blood-combat, & slain again, the beast-within-the beast, wading through its own entrails w/ all the righteous selfsufficiency of a plague, but life must be more than apocalyptic harangue.

The teleological beast has nowhere to go, nowhere to turn, that isn't a mirror, where the infinite regress bends sinisterly, the defaced light no longer reflects, as if two images colliding from opposite ends of the universe illuminate nothing but the bars of its cage.

And into the gap weaves the itsybitsy spider, hunting flies.

Sobremango winked at it as if, imperceptible to the hidden observer (you), some deep complicity existed between them. In art, he opined, mystification can never be petty enough. We're all Arachnians, hanging by a rope or by a thread, authoring our own bondage, conspiring in our doom. What then is art?

It was at this stage that the projector cut out & w/ it the wall of bougainvillea. A commotion at the lectern before the lights came up. In the glare of the amphitheatre, Fidelius appeared as fraught as an archaeological artefact in a vitrine. A mumbling Head of Caesar on which the millennia have bestowed an air of unconquered vacuity.

And it was almost getting interesting, gesticulated Carbonara Inverso, to herself, to no-one.

Sobremango might've felt sorrier had he not at the same instant found himself the object of Senhora Epimedia's unsolicited gaze, fixing him across the front row. Twisting in his seat he very narrowly missed ramming into Pontifax, who was leering over Carbonara Inverso's shoulder. *Tchau-tchau!* simpered Pontifax. It wafted over him like a septic toothache.

Christ!

Fidelius was still flapping about among his papers, attempting to restore order by zealous demonstration of the contrary. What the lecture was supposedly about, Sobremango hadn't the foggiest.

POX JULIA

It's the carnival! The Roman festival! The big parade! The cavalcade! Watch the procession of Caesar's slaves & concubines! Flower-haired children! Vestal virgins! Senator's wives! Priests! Pederasts! Flagellants! Fadistas! Lictors & arselickers! The whole harangued hoi polloi of the local sub-judice, sub-Judaean, subjugated população! And not to be outdone, a couple of notorious inebriates, Butt&Taff-like, eyes heat-glazed, swinging wide w/ flagons in hand, puking onto the cobbles, singing the Great Man's praises, *Oh I was a skivvy on a sinking galley, down in the Mediterranee...* The Legion VII Gemina files past the shopfronts, bombastic centurions posing for the shopgirls. The consul's horse trails dung all along the street. A cassocked priest, beatific smile, w/ left hand slyly groping onlookers' pockets while the right freely distributes blessings. Doves from overhanging eaves cooing. Wreathed in poppy, daffodil & daisy, like topheavy tombstones, the triumphal arches hastily erected in the Praça da República, the faux-Corinthian columns, the plywood ottomans & chaise-longes, the cardboard-cutout merchandising stands. See how the conqueror's standard adorns every lamppost & balcony along the processional route. The fasces of axe & scourge. Brass laurels, spavined eagles, bunting cut from scavenged legionnaire kit, funerary shrouds, brides' nighties. Regard, here, the official brochure, dear reader: pictured, centre, page 3, the valiant steed 'pon which rides the Magistrate Extraordinaire himself, a pair of balls unparalleled in all of Rome, w/ the obvious exception of Caesar's own ("The Pompeian Marbles," fig.2). All hail the Dictator Perpetuo! aka municipal bigwig (bald-as-a-billiard-ball) & Anizar's majordomo, Palhaça Arsénio Salazarini, Presidente da Câmara Municipal, SPQA. There he sits, power incarnate, shifting his chafed backside against the saddle. The adoring masses all have much better things to do than listen to another one of his speeches, they're busy sucking down last year's grapeharvest, mobbing the grill, taking selfies w/ the roast pig. Drums will be banged & horns will be blown. Senhora Epimedia, the carnival's éminence grise, knows the hard part's over & it's all downhill from here. Pretty soon they'll be lying in the gutter or on the steps of Pontifax's ducal palazzo aka Templo Iuno Regina. And look! There's the queen goddess herself, in dishevelled toga, unshaven, squinting from a high balcony, like a Pope ogling the masses of Piazza San Pietro. Where she keeps her auguries is nobody's business. Were there a Rembrandt to record the scene in the true depths of chiaroscuro this noontide forebodes, it'd be a who's who of the city's dramatis personae. They're all here, every last one of them, smiling at the cameras, skulking under awnings, slurping wine, spinning around the maypole, slapping their neighbour's arse, stepping over dead soldiers, stuffing their faces w/ chargrill, spewing behind marquees, slipping on banana skins, screwing in the backs of carriages, singing from rooftops, sopping-up the sauce, swinging from signposts, somersaulting off the bandstand for shits & giggles.

Have you ever seen such a thing in yr life? (Caesar to Epimedia.)

Truly the people love their Caesar! (Epimedia to Caesar.)

Don't be a horse's arse. Just make sure the photos come out.

CANIS CANEM EDIT

First the cocks, then the waking dogs, then the cat's meow, then trash collectors rummaging through the butt-ends of sleep, then floor slapping the face of the one who lies there habitually, when not hung on a wall. Hello beautiful!

6:00am. Albufarkas groped blindly up off the door that, laid horizontal across two breezeblocks, did service as his "monk's palliasse" – most bearable he'd known, please note – gulped coffee dregs direct from the pot & staggered out to the throneroom for his morning stool. The easing of the bowels, Albufarkas considered philosophically, being the most rewarding part of any given day. It gives one everything to look forward to, he professed aloud. His alterego lay in the bathtub, which was too short by several feet, knees up, bare soles resting flat on the floral wall-tiles, thumbing through Albufarkas' manuscript:

You hardly mention me at all, he complained.

Can't a man shit in peace?

Nature, Antifarkas mocked, abhors a pacifist.

As it abhorred Descartes.

Why don't you call it, *Forgotten Loonies of the Great Tradition*? Or *Silhouettes of Blind Ignorance*? Or, how about, *The Age of Enlightenment was a Lie, All as Dark as Ever Was, Future Bright Only Because Approaching at Great Velocity*?

It isn't concerned w/ any of those things.

So what? A persuasive title's half the work.

Since when do you read?

I don't, I absorb. Like ectoplasm. By the way, what's this

bit supposed to mean? *Gritamos. Lançamos. Falhamos. Nós não somos, no entanto, os mesmos. (Por que é que você se está a desculpar?) Eu vejo o verão através da janela. O que vem depois é tristeza. Dizemos: é preciso ser forte. Minha querida, você já foi um cachorro? Ou um filho único? Está na hora de mais um episódio de "Envelhecendo sem graça." Amanhã não é ontem. Esses ensaios são muito fáceis. Eu ouço a multidão. Os lugares vazios. Meu povo! Tranquilo! O que está acontecendo aqui? Eu amo vocês também, mas é o suficiente?*

How shld I know? Albufarkas flushed & observed the Arctic Fresh blue vortex suck his impure self down the wormhole & into outerspace. Or under the floor. Who cared, as long as it stayed there & didn't percolate back to stink out the facilities. On its last legs already as it was. Held together by coprolite for all he knew.

Aren't you afraid yr life's work will end up in the same place?

Where wld you rather it ended up?

Literary fame's no more idiotic than any other ambition.

The ecstatic part about death is it removes all those concerns.

Y're not dead yet, old son, sorry to disappoint. Will let you know when, though. But I perceive a theme developing here. Listen to this: *É a sua vez de morrer comer contar. De manhã, nós fomos doentes. Um pouco. Chove. Um pouco. Quem sou eu? Quem é você? Lembremos outras vozes. Outros amanhãs. A coisa escura está linda na sua mão. Esta ia se a minha vez. (Quem não joga não ganha.) Comíamos a aranha. "Joga xádrez?" Daqui até à prisão é uma curta distância. Comíamos uma outra aranha. Há menos tempo do que eu pensava. O relógio tem oito pernas peludas. "Não se preocupe, esta fase vai passar."* Is this what's connoted by the expression "deathless prose"?

Albufarkas gazed mutely into the reflection of his mouth, undecided about the virtues of finding teeth still in it. Stuck a tube of toothpaste between lips & squeezed. Sucked the goo back & forth a bit. Spat. Gazed a little more. Pearly whites, far from. Well try to imagine a mouth full of drowned-men's eyes, see if that works. Swilled some tapwater. Clacked the choppers together one two three, alas poor Yorick. Cldn't even manage to stay buried, eh, where's the justice in that? Make the punters laugh in this life, end up a butt of morbid ridicule in the next. Or a stageprop, which was worse?

A new chapter: *Time flies like an arrow. Fruit flies like bananas.* Haha. Who'd you steal that from?

Problem w/ enlightenment, even yrs my little friend, is you can only pose a question you already understand how to ask. The truly original question doesn't exist.

Climbed out the peevish side this morning, did we?

Albufarkas rubbed some water on his face. Optimism, he considered, means keeping up the capacity for surprise. Despite knowing better. For example, the person who one morning washes their face off & finds someone else gazing back from the mirror. Cue theatrical astonishment. Well, cld always try bleach. Person one morning erases themselves, astonished to find no longer there. Where's the sense in that? The dispiriting fact is, optimists just liked to go about menacing everyone else w/ their sunny dispositions. Albufarkas wiped his face. Blinked over at his alterego, who was still making a show of perusing.

How many sides does a void have, anyway?

Asking me? Oh here's something: *Is it sick to love a sick mouth?* You know, I'm beginning to detect vaguely autobiographical undertones in all this. For example: *Pare de sofrer, existe uma solução! É amor? O perquisador gosta de observar de longe. Ô que é que ele está fazendo lá? "Que estranho!" Ele acha que o mundo está a chegar ao fim? E daí? (Estou só olhando, obrigado.) Bem, cada pergunta tem seus inimigos. Par exemple, mesmo Deus não é ninguém nesta cidade. (Amor, sem adjectivos.) Vamos supor que em Beja, elas beijam. O bebé chora, o bebé canta. Bebé bebé! Você desliga a luz? Que bom! Ele pede de joelhos. Eu (ass)assino. Eu ensino. Eu agradeço. Longe daqui o prato principal volta das férias. O porco preto é um abacaxi.* Speaking of which, what're the chances of a decent petit déjeuner around here?

I'm tired.

You just woke up.

I woke up a long long time ago, all I want to do now is sleep, like everyone else.

My entire existence is one long bout of insomnia.

I've been meaning to ask, is there only one of you or do you come in multiples?

Unkind, master. Très unkind.

A very singular double, then?

You want the truth?

Never, that wld be foolish.

Just as being singularly duplicitous wld soon be tedious.

Any idiot can tell a lie, but it takes a special kind of idiot not to be able to tell the difference.

According to the Imam, it's idiots all the way down.

And haemorrhoids all the way up.

What's for breakfast?

Albufarkas shrugged out the door. No sooner accomplished than he found himself in the kitchen, eggs boiling clacketyclack on the stove. Voilà! gesticulated Antifarkas. Can't go wrong w/ boiled eggs.

I cld be vegan.

But y're not. I checked in the book. It goes on about Descartes & eggs at irksome length & in excruciating detail, but on the subject of ingesting the humble chicken embryo is in all respects approving. Soft or hard?

Do I look like Schrödinger?

I don't know. What does Schrödinger look like?

Like someone who placed their bet on the wrong animal, I'd imagine. Or three kilograms of ash, take yr pick.

Question is, can you tell the difference between a hard & soft egg w/out breaking them open?

Why not just make an omelette? Sour cream, chives, parmigiana, all there in the fridge. And it's *ovum*, by the way, not *embryo*. Unfertilised. While y're doing that, I'll go & enjoy some peace & quiet in the other room. Alone.

Albufarkas made good his escape, the door firmly wedged behind him, breathing in the dark familiar stink of his sleeping compartment. He groped around for something to wear. Somehow his nakedness had evaded commentary. But then, it occurred to him that his alterego had been naked the entire time also. Cld there be any such thing as a ghoul in its natural state? Thank gob he cldn't see himself, dangling about, most hideous. He dragged on a pair of oversized pants & cinched to the last belt-notch. Still they threatened to abandon at the slightest provocation. Shirt, jacket, boots, fedora. Each gave the impression of having been vacated by a previous tenant. Not possible to slink about in a djellaba, today, lamentably, required to perform certain public ablutions thinkable only in black suit & tie. Even the tie didn't fit. Were it a noose, they'd need to have a second crack at him. Well who says you can't hang the same man twice? Something clanged meanwhile on the balcony. Albufarkas shuffled through the gloom & peered between the shutters. Outside on the narrowest of ledges his alterego was dousing the petunias w/ a watering can, fedora tipped at an angle rakish, shirt collar up-turned, maroon&white beachumbrella in buttonhole. The creature winked.

Whose funeral this time?

Whose funeral this time well what an awful shame it isn't yrs moot point I know but have you considered yr purpose in life questionmark.

Ah! The free indirect style.

Nothing's free.

Ooh! Let it not be said the great man's pessimism was anything but proverbial.

IN CAESAR'S PUDDLE

O Parque Fluvial de Sangue do Rei situa-se a 7 km da cidade de Anizar na Albufeira de Sangue do Rei (com uma área de 50ha), próximo do sítio arqueológico do Império Antigo. Pretende-se que seja uma zona de recreio balnear de eleição, que possibilite ainda a criação de um conjunto de actividades paralelas que promovem o local e permitem tirar partido das potencialidades existentes.

Zona de lazer com areal, palhotas e espreguiçadeiras. É reconhecida como Praia Acessível para pessoas com mobilidade reduzida. Possui um centro de atividades náuticas, parque infantil e embarcadouro. Na envolvente da albufeira existe um circuito de manutenção.

Bar de petiscos com produtos regionais e apoio às restantes actividades. Possui instalações sanitárias e posto de primeiros socorros. Venha desfrutar deste oásis no coração do Alentejo!

DEATH OF A CROW

PLEASE KEEP A SAFE DISTANCE FROM OTHER PEOPLE, read the sign at the entrance to the Casa Mortuária. The place was filthy w/ black polyester & gabardine. Fly-eyed under mantillas & sunglasses. Just how many had death undone? The mourners stood, armed w/ their solemnity, like a sinister chorusline about to mortify themselves w/ olive branches & cante alentejano.

Albufrakas approached the gauntlet in unmasked trepidation. Wld he or wld he not? What day was it? Thursday: five-in-yr-eye to blind the beast. Florida there in the shadows by the gate hawking her charms on the hush-hush. Albufarkas, eyeing her up, felt a malevolent glare directed at the back of the head.

What's that frigging yid doing coming to a place like this in broad daylight?

Albufarkas recognised the dulcet tones of Princess Legerdemain's sottovoce. He's one of THEM! Carbonara Inverso sniggered.

Ah, sighed Albufarkas' alterego, the eternal bearing of crosses. *Der ewige Jude!*

Albufarkas felt himself being gradually surrounded & borne along by the swelling crowd. Barely 7:00am & already the hoi polloi waking the dead. Sobremango's personal menagerie were filing past the evil eyes like so many apparitions in a mirror maze who, having caught sight of themselves, started to flee pellmell under the lychgate, to the general consternation of those marooned on the other side.

From the frying pan into the fire, lisped Antifarkas.

Behind him, meanwhile, Legerdemain was gossiping to Senhora Epimedia.

We heard about [inaudible] from Vitor Domingo, who was walking w/ him from the Santo Amaro markets, along rua Conselheiro Meneses, when apparently a blind old man, w/ corneas that made his eyes slate-grey, stopped them as they crossed the street, a classic Alentejo gypsy all in black, w/ a black scarf & a black felt hat, & it over 40 degrees in the shade, & the old blindman latched onto [inaudible]'s arm & asked wld he direct him to the cemetery as he was late for a funeral, & of course [inaudible] not being hard-hearted obliged the old gypsy & that was the last Vitor Domingo or anyone else ever saw of him.

The hodgepodge congregation filed into the chapel where undertakers had laid out a most ex-officio Palhaça Arsénio Salazarini, Head Honcho (past-tense) of the República Pax-Julia, in a closed casket surmounted by a 6ft-square portrait of the deceased's mimesis, laurel wreath upon dauntless Caesarian brow, rhinophymic nose, pronounced strabismus, buckteeth, thyroid cartilage, copious chest-rug overspilling from tunic, purple toga resplendent, in a frame of black crepe. There was a jockeying for position to get the best or worst view, stomping on electric candles, causing the neatly stacked prayerbooks to totter lasciviously.

Ladies & gentlemen please!

A midget in borrowed cassock scuppered about uselessly flapping its wings. The architraves wheezed as the crowd spewed in. Albufarkas wasn't unduly surprised to glimpse Imam Koan seated above the ruckus at the chapel's pipeorgan in greased-down hair & black aviators auguring faint strains of Bach out of the pneumatic contraption. The strains undulated. Swirled. Resolved into a precise mathematical order. Soon the masses were as sheep in a corral. It was rumoured Koan was the Princess's hitman-manqué, he'd bicycle around town w/ a violin case managing her affairs, apparently.

The pew Albufarkas found himself presently occupying sank precariously under a collective weight as the unshriven squeezed in ear-to-ear. Organ music soared. Crystalline facets of subject & countersubject. Like being consumed & spat out by pure dialectics. Faint stirrings of a migraine as Albufarkas gazed down between caked shoes, sweating under black felt. Tipped himself slightly forward, so that the brim of said fedora, conspicuously unremoved, rested atop the seatback in front, forehead crease pressed directly into woodgrain, producing a slight dull anaesthesia, so as to brace himself against the effects of gravity & interminable monologue, shld he thus surrender his consciousness during the priest's sermon. All things being imminent.

So Albufarkas found himself eye-to-eye, in a manner of speaking, w/ some misfortunate spider that'd been varnished inbetween the floorboards. Like a fly in amber. Hahaha. Not so *komisch* for the spider, though.

Which wld you rather be?

Well to be honest sunshine I reckon there's still a fighting chance of making a comeback from the present positional disadvantage without turning myself into an objet d'art.

Antifarkas pulled a face:

Speak for yrself darling.

What?

Don't you ever get bored pretending to be spontaneous in a situation like this, w/ that posthumous momzer glopping down at us? Who does he think he is, anyway, Big Brother's cousin third-removed?

It's a social ritual, everyone has their part to play.

Y're the next best thing to a pariah in this town, that's the only part anyone expects you to play.

Exactly.

You think y're building an alibi?

I don't need an alibi.

Everyone needs an alibi. The minute they open their mouths, before they've even learnt to breathe, they're already rehearsing a line of defence.

Why does everything you say end up sounding like déjá vu, hahaha?

Perhaps because I'm yr alterego & everything I say comes out of yr head?

You mean I know everything y're going to say before you say it?

Knowledge isn't always conscious. Just because y're cognate w/ the saying doesn't mean y're aware of it until it happens. Because every saying is a repetition of something you only know in anticipation. A re-*cognition*. Y'd know what I'm going to say whether I said it or not. Or whether you were aware of it or not.

The priest, who'd made his presence known to the congregation, announced his intention to discourse on the subject of remembrance, embarking upon his perorations while Albufarkas, hunched in his pew, mumbled not inaudibly, in confirmation to his oppressed neighbours that this queer interloper was indeed cracked. A kind of symmetry was thereby established, one that was easily anticipated & in no way unnatural, disconcerting, spooky, conspiratorial. The theme of remembrance had a very high probability of arising at some point during any given funeral service, in direct proportion to a collective desire to disremember, erase, blankout, forget. It was the sort of thing that might've been referred to as a chestnut, though Albufarkas cld recall only a single gaunt representative of the species from all his wanderings through Anizar, casting its withered shade across the entrance of the Rainha Dona Leonor Museum. Perhaps the point of a chestnut was to be metaphorical rather than literal. The sermoniser appeared deliberately to avoid the slightest resolution of this dilemma. It was the kind of oration designed to instil a sense of futility, fatalism & false hope. Like the consubstantiation. Or a mental deficiency one is forced to simulate under pain of eternal undeath. *Blessèd is he who perseveres through trial blah blah.* For he shall reap in abundance the suffering due to those incapable of learning a lesson the first time around.

Tubs of morally righteous eyewash, quipped Antifarkas.

Heads turned to see what it was about, but catching sight of the oddbod in the black felt hat turned immediately away again. Unable to participate in their pointofview, Albufarkas conjured this image of himself, as in a dream, cracking & peeling the shell of an enormous lacquered egg. A spider's egg bigger than a pterodactyl's. Rolling it Sisyphus-like up the aisle as all the chapel's inhabitants looked-on, gobsmacked, then letting it roll back down again. Crack. One piece at a time. Crackcrack. Till a revealed sack of ambered albumin in which his alterego lay coiled foetuslike gazing w/ hugely expressive eyes up at the martyred Christ crucified against Koan's pipeorgan, Bach resurgent. And this vision suddenly & inexplicably brought to Albufarkas' aching mind a piece of great culinary wisdom passed down from his dearest longlost Matka while still in his infancy. The art, his mother used to say, rocking his bundle w/ her foot while gazing intensely at a pot of water on the unlit stove, is in convincing the egg y've boiled it, w/out having to resort to such actual violence.

CAVEAT EMPTOR

The fleamarket was dogs on fleabitten blankets coiled into the bricàbrac. Mouldy clocks telling mouldy time. Louche lemonade bottles & libertine lotus-blossom faux chandeliers. A ménage of streetsweepers stand off to one side ogling the rubbish, their overseer waving a brocaded shirtsleeve at distant prospects of urban renewal. Cleanliness was first next to godliness. And wld God himself one day from on high smile beatifically down upon their solemnly bared heads as they beat dust-dervishes out of birch brooms? Desultory waterspouts hiss & belch in the pond round which the vendors have set out their wares. Swallows dart through the spray. Disorientated pigeons wade ever-tentative among the algae. A not-at-all-tentative drunk lies w/ broiled feet lapping at the suds. As once upon a time wildebeest & flamingo in their evolutionary swamp hypnotised by the unblinking crocodile. There are no moments, they seem to say, only eternities. The sellers of profundity sit under lean-tos fanning themselves prodigiously, feigning to ignore any stray browser that bungles past till coming within reach, at which point: better to avert one's gaze. See how the traffic drags itself along the adjacent avenue w/ a manic sunstruck glint of eye? And there strides Albufarkas w/ his dogsbody hat & tin watering can. What the hell does he expect to accomplish w/ a thing like that in a place like this?

El Pontifax waved a persistent fly from the bridge of his tuberous nose. It was said that once in a moment of egregious spite, he'd crammed his buttocks out a window of the Temple of Jupiter & shat on the unfortunate supplicants below. That, of course, was a filthy lie. Never in yr own nest – he sneezed, not bothering to cover a mouth overflowing w/ rotten dentistry – nor out of it either. Was there any point to ceremony these days? I have only one thing to say on the matter – again sneezed, again the riot of orthodontics – which is, that it's ridiculous to say God is dead, since He can never have lived in the first place. Not in the sense of a mensch capable of being nailed to a cross. Had it been otherwise, the resurrected body of Christ wld simply be a miracle of nature, like a Galapagos turtle. Thus in one fell swoop the Pontifax obliterated the dogmas.

I'm inclined to *believe otherwise*, stated Princess Legerdemain, in observance of the retreating figure avec scarecrow's fedora & irrigation appliance, else how wld it be possible to explain stupidity?

Perhaps it isn't. Most probably it isn't. If it was, it wld've been explained long before now.

The two babblers were stretched out on a public bench, as was their wont when the taking-in of la condition humaine made demands upon their undivided attention. In such posture they were the proverbial Pécuchet & Bouvard.

Notice, however, persisted the princess, that Galapagos turtles exist.

But does stupidity really exist? Or is it just a kind of illusion, like politics?

There are days when the elements are, to put it plainly, by & large unsympathetic to the labours of intellection & this was one of them. The streetsweepers, their overseer by now having retreated to an airconditioned sub-office, were fast catching some shut-eye under the eucalypts. Pontifax immediately thought to do the same. These creatures, he intoned, have understood the true meaning of our place in the universe: we are merely the camponês of entropy. He then tilted back his overbite into the first octave of a rising snore.

Eh wake the fuck up! Legerdemain thumped him in the bicep w/ her fist. You expect me to sit here & suffer on my lonesome?

Suffering's overrated, he yawned, shaking his head, but not too vigorously, so as to avoid unintended consequences. I speak from long experience. When I was young I had a great talent for it. At school I'd frequently be called upon to demonstrate the correct technique. I knew even then that a promising career lay before me & that all I needed to do was allow my natural abilities to develop unimpeded. I was a vocational guidance counsellor's dream. How else d'you think I ended up in this business?

I hadn't given it the slightest thought at all, why wld I?

Florida, a grrl-child in a widow's mantilla, had been eavesdropping on this exchange from behind a stall festooned in the zinc, turquoise & Klein Blue of the Evil Eye, & was by now in transports of incredulity. She stamped her diminutive foot on the hot cobbles: Don't either of you realise there's a war going on?

There's always a war going on, honey, yawned Pontifax copiously. It's one of the few certainties in life.

It isn't right, for you to be lounging there w/ all yr palaver while innocents die.

And you hawking superstitious idols! scoffed Legerdemain. Shldn't you be in school?

School's for numbskulls, Florida pouted. Life is the true teacher.

Ah, life! Pontifax waved a moist paw in the hot immobile air. To be or not to be, that is the verb. As for the noun, well yr guess is as good as mine.

Oh really, Florida let out a sigh, I don't know if I even belong in this world.

You & me both, darling. Sometimes I don't even know if I'm Joan of Arc or the Wizard of Oz.

That's easy for you to say, snorted Legerdemain, y're a natural-born catastrophe.

Ain't nothing natural about me, sweetness, except my personality, the rest was bought w/ hard currency.

You never bought a thing in yr life!

The secret to doing business is never spending yr own money.

I think I chose the wrong line of approach, Florida fingered one of the blue & white trinkets hanging on her stall. People screamed for less. Wld screaming help? I don't know what to do w/ my life, she thought, w/out saying it. Think it don't say it was her grandma's maxim which she'd uttered w/out fail every day of her life it seemed, except that Florida's grandma had passed away the previous autumn & perhaps the absence of this font of wisdom was the true source of the grrl-child's distress.

Whose junk is that anyway? Legerdemain feigned interest.

Senhor Fidelius, no less. She's the prodigal daughter.

You don't say? Is this where he fences his dodgy artefacts?

They're supposed to ward off evil spirits, doncha know?

Evidently doesn't work.

Speak for yrself, Legs.

I'd be better off as a robot, sulked Florida.

That's it, kiddo, always look on the bright side.

Or nothing, Florida shrugged. Why be anything when y're bound to be disappointed? This is what the school of life has taught me so far.

Easiest thing in the world finding a reason to not do something.

A day will come, intoned Pontifax. A voice from the sky.

Life is so meaningless.

Reason prevails even where meaning is lacking.

Y're all optimism today, Legs, what's the matter?

I need a drink is what's the matter.

What about the kid?

Let her sweat it out.

At that moment some indeterminate foreigners slouched past, speaking in tongues. Pontifax squirmed on the bench, moaning as if he'd been suddenly stricken w/ appendicitis. Argh, why'd G.O.D. have to go & invent other languages? Aren't there enough mumbling halfwits in the world to begin w/, was it necessary to create more?

THE SELFMADE WOMXN

Tonight they commemorate w/ barrage upon barrage of incendiary balloons, bombing down over the city into a tinder landscape, the pioneering spaceflight of the first womxn cosmonaut? No? Well then almost. Behind every god-on-Earth stands a mother willing to pick up the pieces, to wipe up the faeces, to doctor the photographs? No? Well what part shld choice play in anything, when it comes down to it, y're either born w/ wings or y're not? No? Well let them all burn & see who rises to the top...

Florida: Well Jesus Christ didn't have much of a father, but Senhora Maria cld fly like a witch!

Imam Koan: The witch flies or the broomstick?

Florida: Einstein says gravity's a fictional force. What's flight?

Imam Koan: An overcoming of resistance.

Florida: Rape by any other name.

Imam Koan: Was Maria raped by Yahweh?

Florida: Ectopic pregnancies exist & can be fatal.

Imam Koan: Yet is it possible to abort an idea, even from necessity?

Florida: If the conditions that give rise to an idea are real, can its death be a fiction?

Imam Koan: Or anything but?

Florida: The true causes aren't always the ones we think.

Imam Koan: Like world socialism.

Florida: To love yr neighbour means to love all yr neighbours equally or risk complications.

Imam Koan: Vive la révolution sexuelle!

Florida: Cld Jesus have been a woman?

Imam Koan: Herod's gaol was no convent.

Florida: Or Joseph?

Imam Koan: All things being equal.

Florida: Or the Magdalene a man?

Imam Koan: Do you know the Barber of Savile Row?

Florida: Opera attire always seems like too much work.

Imam Koan: Labour redeems.

Florida: Also concentration camps.

Imam Koan: Music transcends suffering.

Florida: Bollocks!

Imam Koan: "May love & faith eternally reign!"

Florida: My love is like an umbrella to yr farce.

Imam Koan: It's said the Nazarene walked upon the water, not under it.

Florida: He cld've driven a U-boat for all I care.

Imam Koan: Give me a virgin & a snorkel any day.

Florida: Does life even have a point or are we just evolution's afterthought?

Imam Koan: Meaning attaches to things through experience.

Florida: Yrs or mine?

Imam Koan: Theirs.

Florida: Does natural selection have a mind of its own, then?

Imam Koan: Any system can be a neural network.

Florida: Intelligent design?

Imam Koan: Do you know why you think what y're thinking while y're thinking it?

Florida: Reverse engineering?

Imam Koan: Perhaps the Angelus Novus had a two-way mirror.

Florida: That'd mean coming already prepared.

Imam Koan: Time's all about narrowing the odds even as the possibilities multiply out of hand.

Florida: Insider trading. Bribery & corruption.

Imam Koan: What good's divinity if it doesn't keep an ace in the hole?

Florida: If the world were a level playing field, everything wldn't be going downhill.

Imam Koan: A flat Earth in one dimension is a doughnut in another.

Florida: I've never seen Berlin.

Imam Koan: Irving, those days were among my fondest.

Florida: Anything you can do...

Imam Koan: Even equality has to draw the line somewhere.

Florida: Is there no hope for us, then?

Imam Koan: Hope is for the hopeless as need is for the needless.

Florida: I am that I am, what good are concepts?

Imam Koan: They cost nothing but can be sold for a fortune.

Florida: It always comes down to money in the end.

Imam Koan: The end's the one place money never is.

Florida: I'd like to go there one day.

Imam Koan: Fair to say it's on the cards.

Florida: Do you cast horoscopes as well?

Imam Koan: I fancied myself in the movie business, once upon.

Florida: Hollywood?

Imam Koan: Katz's All You Can Peep.

Florida: Quelle delicatesse!

UM BANHO CHEIO DE MULHERES

Legerdemain pursed garishly rouged lips & spat a mouthful of coffee grounds back into her cup. Merde alors! From her spot on the terrace she had a clear view of the runt in the tangerine one-piece w/ little sharkfin tits jabbing out. A Max Beckmann travesty, languidly inviting violence. How gratifying if she cld just stick out a leg, hook a hefty calf behind the runt's neck & reel in! Half-starved thing. Be like a cat at a tin of briny Minerva. Jesus I'll melt! The princess let a not-insubstantial fist fall to the tabletop. THIS AIN'T COFFEE she raged, at a schoolboy waiter in his starched bib. Misfortune had brought him within reach. IT'S GODDAM *EF-FLUENT*! The runt turned to take in the commotion. Caught the little prissy's eye? There, that did the trick! What a choice piece of confectionery. I'd do her, solemnised the princess' inner-arbiter, before the fizz dries on my spit. Senhora, senhora! The idiot in the big baby's bib. Brushed aside brusquement w/ gaudy beringed flab-fingers, If y're expecting me to pay for *that* you can kiss my farts. She's already halfway across the deck, locking the tangerine runt in a cunt-withering stare. The waiter ogles. Protective mothers rush instinctively to their young & smother them in terrytowelling. The runt grins back a vague, slovenly grin. Retracts knees to sharkfin torso. Lets slip akimbo one blushing thigh. Legerdemain's precipitant progress across the poolside, arrested by a sudden laryngeal obstruction. There follows ungainly fits of hoiking & coughing. Undulations of blue taffeta. By fuck if the runt doesn't have the biggest cock she's ever seen. Hahaha the magpies cackle. Peekabooing children giggle. Legerdemain rights her keel, pats red cheeks, tilts coiffure at an angle sinister. Heels-toes forward. My oh my. Prazer em conhecê-la! Unctuously. Come here often, mmm? Winks all-round. Hooo-aaah.

Legerdemain yawned, stirred from her reverie on the sweatsoaked deckchair by who-knows-what, swatted a mosquito from her ear. Bugger, always just when it was about to get interesting. Oh! Smirking straight across the pooldeck at her was Pablo Bandera, putative revolutionary, in a pair of red&black speedos. As always, he trailed a retinue of bearded young men, unaccustomed to sunlight. Bandera paused, flexed his hips, wafted a Cuban cigar at some future vision of socialist utopia buried in conspiratorial shade beneath a linden tree. The retinue departed for this promised land. Bandera winked. It sent shivers up Legerdemain's spine. Were Bandera's swimming pool conspiracy ever to ascend the heights of municipal power, she cld be certain of being, if not the first, at least among those closely affiliated, to be put against the wall. Which wall precisely being open to debate, but there was no shortage. Odds-on she'd get it in the neck right next to El Pontifax, maybe they'd even make it an ensemble. Petacci & Mussolini. Hang their dogsbodies from the diving tower by the same rope. Edifying thought. Well, dearies, there cld always be sorrier ways. The Kadyrovtsi were known to castrate their victims *en avant*. Among other pleasantries. Let's not. Moot, you say? Why quibble over details at this early stage? And so many other fish in the sea waiting to be fried.

With panoptic gaze the princess cast around for compensation (life can't be all misery & politics!). The vision splendid was not in short supply. All those lithe sons & daughters of, rushing to go to waste. Y're a hag even before you bleed in a hellhole like this. Mon dieu! And oh dear Christ, here comes Dona Cinquenta, that prurient old cunt, in a withered two-piece wedged ostentatiously up her crack. Have they no dignity? It's not that I mind getting old, but the spectacle of it, my god! Like keeping a seat warm in a mummy's tomb. All those painted nabobs parading about naked on the walls w/ sagging eggcup tits endlessly in profile as if all they ever did in life was sidle up to one another begging for a dose of crabs while Nubian slaves fan the hothouse air & Anubis counts his shekels at the door. Y'd have to suppose if the sly dog had a mind to he cld've extorted a piece of overbaked arse or two for a quick jig around the underworld without the usual eternity of bureaucratic foreplay. Fancy being jacked-off by Death's own gigolo, hahaha! Well they do say every dog has its day, hahaha! And bom dia to you, too, Dona Cinquenta! Sim, Dona Cinquenta! Muito obrigada, Dona Cinquenta! Now there was a legend, Legerdemain reminded herself, that, after the war, in which, needless to say, the Estado Novo played no part, a delegation of the women of Anizar, & Dona Cinquenta among them, marched upon the Municipal Palace to submit a non-negotiable demand to the powers-that-be, that an open-air bathing facility be constructed for the benefit of all humxnity, upon this very spot & post-haste, under pain of unspecified consequences of a rumouredly conjugal nature, etc. (Ah, & wasn't Dona Cinquenta herself, Anizar's own liposuctioned Lysistrata, the prizest piece of rat bait those Novo Estadistas had ever clapped their occulars on?) Uff! Thus was water struck from stone (or at least reinforced concrete) without a moment's compromise to Anizar's net reproductive rate, au contraire! Many a sodden sunburnt hallelujah was thereby sung. Let us give thanks, in any case. Were it not for those illustrious women of Anizar, might she herself, the very peerless Princess Legerdemain, at this very moment not be stuck cooling her jambs at some filthy soakhole out in the peripheral wilderness, where even the great unwashed feared to tread? Perish the thought. And what, for her part, had she, the aforesaid Legerdemain, given in return to the Dona Cinquentas of the world, but her priceless disdain? Well now, beggars can't be choosers, can they sweetbits?

Neck craned over the back of her deckchair, Legerdemain contemplated Dona Cinquenta's posterior as it wended its retreating way across the thronged terrace. Riddance! Casually, so as not to jinx herself, she scanned for runts. Scant luck. A gaggle of insalubrious jejunes waddled out of the café – tablesful of humxn colostomy bags swilled SuperBock &

swatted flies – rows of halfbaked spring chickens lolled about on deckchairs bathed in almond milk & coconut oil – here & there pederasts in aviators & Hawaiian shirts heavily perspiring under gaudy beach umbrellas, like hanging up a shopsign. Well, came a familiar voice just wafting into earshot from the northeast, I'll tell you... It was, so strike her dumb, the voice of the people's poet, Sobremango no less, schlepping out from under the lindens in towel & flipflops, accompanied by (Legerdemain strained to detect) *une femme d'un certain âge* (incognita, presently) festooned like a piña colada.

Then all of a sudden Carbonara Inverso, too, came within range.

My dear, Carbonara Inverso spluttered loudly at Sobremango, I simply *must* tell you what happened in my office this morning.

Oh tell me all!

Yes dearest (Senhora Piña Colada), you must!

Well, it was like this.

The three of them skirted behind Legerdemain who, under enormous flophat & Sofia Loren shades, was practically invisible. The princess moaned. It was obvious the Sobremango Gang intended to pile around a table & blather away for hours. At some point you have to draw the line. She began to hoist herself off the deckchair when a strap broke & her left tit fumbled out. Holy hell! She reconfigured, taking stock of the situation. Better to wait it out, just in case, you never knew, being accosted while in a compromising position, etc. Legerdemain wrenched at her towel & draped it over the offending region.

So I was sharing coffee w/ my newest secretary when this variety act barged into the office demanding a spot on the programme. One of those family troupes w/ a dog. Mother father daughter son. What happens when no-one's guarding the inner sanctum, apparently, but who on Earth comes barging in at eight a.m.?

Tut-tut.

Well you can hardly blame the secretary.

First day on the job, was it?

I was just easing her in, getting her comfortable in the new surroundings, showing her the ropes, mmm?

Bad luck, poor creature, to be invaded right off the bat.

They were horrible, too. Like a pack of Jehovah's Witnesses duffed-up in their Sunday horrors. I told them straight off, we don't do family acts, zero interest, can't pay people to watch that sort of crap. But we're different, the father of them said. No-one's fucking different, I said. Just let us show you & then decide, he said. The kind of smug pasty-faced sonofabitch makes you want to scream. I had to pinch my new little asset to get her into action, flapping about in a doomed effort to usher Swiss Family Robinson out the door. But these types only respond more intractably to being manhandled & Doris wasn't anywhere near up to the task, sad to say, so before I cld even dial the lummox up at the concierge's desk there they were, stripped starkers on my burgundy Moroccan pile, going at it hell-for-leather like Roman senators.

Eh? Including the dog?

Including the dog.

And what about yr poor secretary?

Stood there taking notes like it was an induction course.

Shorthand or long?

My secretary's hands, dearest, are perfection itself, it isn't about her *hands*.

Did you film them at least?

Yr interlopers, she means.

Alas, I was too caught up in the situation.

So what shld we infer transpired?

Oh what *didn't* transpire? You wldn't believe. I've never seen. It was quite indescribable. A complete bloodbath. The atmosphere. You cld hardly breathe!

And all this before my breakfast time.

Well, then?

I must admit, I was speechless.

That's all?

Come, come, do tell.

What can I say? At the end they were all very eager for appraisal. Stood there on the carpet & bowed. Even the dog bowed. Secretary actually applauded, the nitwit. I, on the other hand, maintained a strictly professional demeanour.

Of course you did.

Keep 'em guessing's what I always say.

I smiled politely. Instructed my secretary to return their apparel & take their details. The usual. Indicated that, shld anything open up, we'd call. Stirred cold coffee. Waited for them to get the fuck out of my office. But it seemed they weren't going to leave until I said *what* I thought of their act. That's all anyone cares about these days, likes likes likes. It's virtually obligatory. They were making those baleful puppy eyes, it was enough to cause any self-respecting humxn to throw up. The children ogled me w/ particular indecency. The dog lolled its tongue. I had no choice but to give in. It's certainly a novel approach, I offered. Rather niche. Has definite potential, though. A really gutsy performance. Credit where credit's due. In the end, I cldn't help myself, I mean, what the hell do you call something like that? Well what *do* you call it, I said. They all blinked back like it was the stupidest question they'd ever heard. Silence. Then the daughter, blushing, squeaked out: Everyone calls it THE COMMUNISTS.

But I don't get it! (Senhora Piña Colada)

That cld be the point, dearest.

D'you suppose it's a comment on the current parlous state of our democracy?

It's the end of the world as we know it!

Climate catastrophe! Pandemic! War! Spiralling inflation! Energy crisis! Orgies on the carpet!

The road of excess & the Palace of Wisdom!

Capitalism's dead, but cld this be something worse?

The poison or the cure?

Rome didn't burn in a day, you know.

Pablo Bandera's scarlet&black speedos suddenly reappeared, obstructing the entirety of Legerdemain's field-of-vision, which had the not unwelcome effect of distracting from Sobremango's inane repartee. (She only hoped, for his readership's sake, that the people's poet didn't write his own books. Not that she was one to judge, she'd never so much as sullied a page. Who read books anyway? Literature was really just psychological class warfare. Plato denounced literature because he was an earnest prole, the archetypal roundhead. Whereas the sonnet was invented so the barons wld be preoccupied w/ their sensibilities & not their swords.)

Vive la révolution!

Bandera's crotch swayed like an incitement to a crosseyed bull.

Legerdemain's eyes spiralled vertiginously in their sockets.

Round & round the garden, what a blinding pair! One step, twostep, tickly under there?

She, Legerdemain, feeling the effects of a hot flush, of the onset of hyperventilation, of a pronounced dizziness, of a vague but increasingly (& quite rapidly so) acute peristalsis, made a sudden involuntary lurch. In the course of which:

Sobremango's repartee got sucked back inside his open mouth;

Piña Colada belched;

Bandera, nonchalantly widestanced, smirked.

With all the tragicomic grace of a panicked walrus in full rut, Legerdemain, twisting her beachtowel into an over-torqued knot of queer intricacy, jackknifed facefirst (at the very instant of eruption from her bulimic buccal cavity (100% Brazilian Arabica)) into Bandera's anarchosyndicalist bikini.

And scored a bullseye.

LOBO EM BOLO

It comes down to the optics of it. One thing seen, another thing believed. Eyes sliding down the menu encounter... Garfo&Faca – €2.95? (Like a pair of farctrocious farnarkelers at a Eurovision Song contest.) A certain kind of establishment, then. A certain ethos. Perhaps they were intended to be keepsakes? You paid for the knives & forks, & even the glasses, plates, napkins, tablecloth, table, chairs, the salt & pepper shakers, the oil & vinegar, & took them all w/ you when you left? A brisk business in kitchenware. Or else ancient custom dictated that eating be done solely w/ the hands, cutlery amounting to a profanation. Like drinking from a fingerbowl at Buckingham Palace, hahaha. God save the dear dead Queenie & all that. But is to tax profanity not thereby to profit from it? Fine, they say, that'll be extra. You wanna park in the handicapped zone, cough up. The food poisoning's free.

Thus Albufarcas mumbling into his plate, to whose contents he seemed desirous to communicate. And struggled to do so for some time. The state of the tablecloth indicated he'd already been at it a while before the narrative chanced to take an interest in him. Deep within the confusion of his eyes one might've detected a profound literary embolism. But this isn't the case here, Albufarkas is just an ex-drunk unable to operate utensils.

Seated at the next table, Antifarkas sardonically bears witness. A sorry sight. At least let a man masticate in peace.

Of course, well, if you call that *masticating*. Gleeking his prayers, maybe. Seeking forgiveness of the omnivarious tablecloth, metonymy of all tablecloths, at all times & in all places where culinary establishments are to be found, from the lowest to the highest, in this life & the next. Wld it be fair to say that Antifarkas is taking liberties w/ the authorial point-of-view? Let us concede, were our distressed diner to expropriate the tableware & drape himself in it, morsel of charred porco preto pasted to brow, filleted frango filligreeing his shirtfront, olive-oiled eyeglasses, chewed coriander sprigs dangling from cauliflower ears, beard besmirched w/ battered breadcrumbs, eggyolked fedora, a vestige of dignity might almost be restored. A certain beatitude, in a sundry shaft of reflected sunlight coming off a swinging glass door. A certain solemnity, even. As w/ rabbinical cast of eye he turns to his alterego & blows a resounding raspberry.

As anyone can deduce, the true story behind Albufarkas' tashlich ablutions is extremely long & complex, so it's only reasonable in the present circumstances to ruthlessly compress.

Albufarkas' favoured lunchtime special may likewise be described as *economical.* Even so, he avoided the cutlery surcharge w/ a determination verging on fanaticism.

It wasn't that, in the art of table manners, he had bad teachers, only trivial ones.

Dessert was on the house.

O TRUQUE DA VIDA
VIVE-LA O RESTO?
FUCK ARRANJA-SE...
YOU SYSTEM IM
MONEY
MONEY
MONEY

CARLOS M. DE ALMEIDA
ASSISTÊNCIA TÉCNICA
RÁDIO TV-COR VÍDEO
SOM ALTA FIDELIDADE

ALCOCHETE
PROMOTOR:
TOIROS E TAUROMAQUIA, LDA.
NIF:
Apoio
Município
de Alcochete

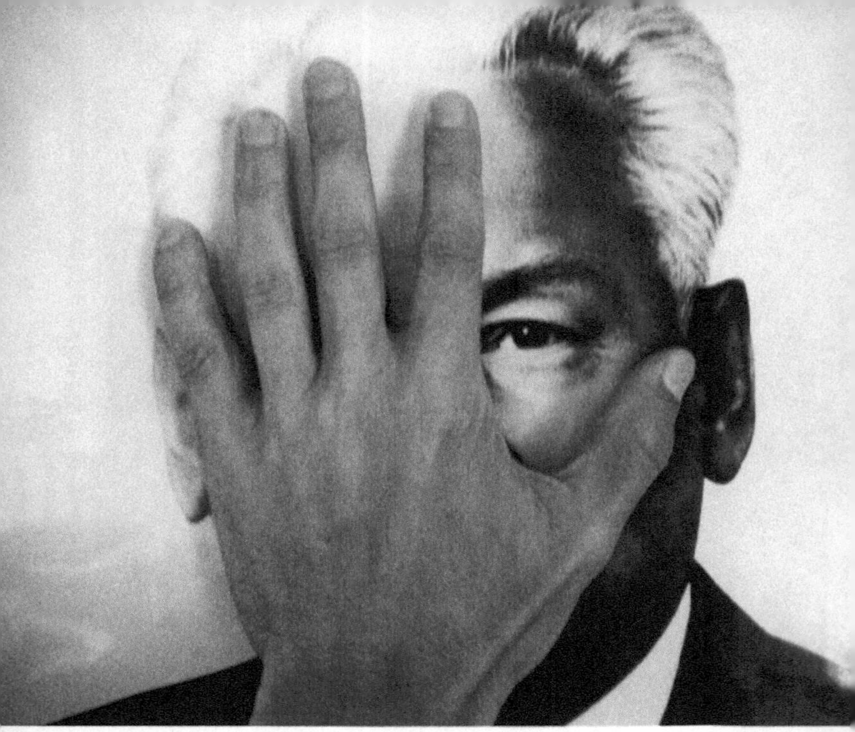

THE TEMPLE OF JUNO

Another lacerating exercise in purgation was waiting for them behind the barred gate. No possible mimesis cld do it justice, it required to be directly suffered. To become one flesh in a state of turmoil, the inner w/ the outer. Rubbish of this kind incanted hallucinogenically in the brains of the celebrants as they filed in, dragging the crimson hems of their togas over a carpet of cigarette butts, empty bottles, playstation consoles. A mannequin's legs protruded from an oversized plantpot wreathed in plastic fern. Someone had stuck a miniature glow-in-the-dark Blessèd Virgin to one of the mannequin's footsoles.

Though he'd just come out of the blazing sun, Caesar Salazarini wore a dozen yards of purple calico draped over a dark suit & tie, flanked by two cronies in black fedoras, red neckerchiefs & a pair of ransacked bedsheets. He received the complimentary beverage dispensed at the door by a Nubian in cardboard shackles w/ long-habituated photogeniality as the local paparazzes, all in the Municipality's employ, dutifully snapped. The cronies chugged, followed close behind by the seven representatives of the Advisory Subcommittee of the Baixo Alentejo Regional Archaeological Commission (ASBARAC), costumed as Lusitanian Gauls of dubious stature.

Where oh where is Snow White? quipped Caesar.

Out back, sunning herself by the pool, winked the Nubian, distributing halfglasses of shandy to the dwarfs.

Caesar: Yeah, zat right?

The shandy tasted like regurgitated dog's piss. Y'd have

to've been subhumxn not to take the affront personally. Just one more thing to add to Salazarini' list of grievances. Forcing a diplomatic blankness of expression, he lurched across the atrium & through the green doors, dumping the remainder of the complimentary beverage into a plantpot. The cronies belched, stomped on each other's bedsheets to keep up & mimed a synchronised pratfall for the cameras. The paparazzes bolted after their Boss, leaving the cronies faceplanted among the hydrangeas. The slavegirl giggled.

Down the musty hall, past the balustered staircase, over the fake-marble expanses & out the sliding glass doors, Caesar slouched, following his nose. A melancholic stink more ancient than Rome percolated from the substrate of Pontifax's backyard comingling w/ notes of incinerated hemp. The dwarfs tumbled out the sliding doors close upon the Imperator's heels propelled by photo-fervid papparachiks.

The yard was a bedlam of inebriates. Pontifax, in the unpersuasive disguise of Queen Juno, lay raving on an inflatable chaise longue, very obviously *non compos mentis*. Caesar's retinue ogled their supine host. He appeared to be chomping on the leg of a duck while bellowing the Swiss national anthem, it was difficult to tell. (But was he or was he not an ASBARACer at heart? This was what the dwarf delegation had been sent to ascertain. Wld they? Who cared?) (The paparazzes fired indiscriminately into the crowd hopeful for a frontpage shot.) (Caesar snorted a prole's parody of patrician contempt.) (The cronies pratfell pellmell.)

A pair of vestals floated up from the throng waving mouthspray. *100% pure straight from a Zürich lab.* Ja wohl! Salazarini demurred. If he started hallucinating now there was no telling where it wld end. The dwarfs wasted no time setting to work at the more serious task of consciousness heightening. The papparazes inquired about the state of the vestals' virginity. Salazarini, impervious to further appeals of chimerical enlightenment, pushed past the party priestesses & made straight for the inflatable tub that took up pride of place in the palazzo's dilapidated parterre, paparazzes in tow. There was a bone to be picked. Pontifax lobbed a mauled duckleg.

Cackled. Flashbulbs flashed. It was broad daylight. Pontifax flopped back on his regal lilo.

Caesar Salazarini was convinced this jesting Juno was a congenital horizontalist, so rarely did the creature appear to have a peg to stand on. He stomped across the paving stones, hoist his toga & waded in. Juno Pontifax lay there like a floundering fish reciting the parable of the loaves to lovelorn apostles. Like a Jew-manqué, w/ the voice of a pickpocket (mused the Salazarini standing just over five feet in the sodden bedsheet). Probably used bugspray for deodorant, too, though to no evident effect, there were flies everywhere. Panto Caesarini swatted his way out to the middle of the paddlingpool only to find himself shrouded in new & uncharted depths of obscurity, like the eye of a dipteran storm. Bulbs flashed. Paparazzes peered through flyspecked viewfinders in unaffected awe.

Further description of the scene wld only result in oversimplification.

Suffice it to say that Caesar Salazarini, commanding the centre of this abrupt vortex, & by-now fully indiscernible to the clowns w/ the cameras, sought to salvage the situation by looming large over his erstwhile adversary, insofar as a man barely 5ft tall in a 3ft swimmingpool, blinded by a blizzard of flying insects, is capable of looming over anything at all. None of the Pointifactual retinue exhibited the slightest suspicion of this nonpareil disappearing act. Even Salazarini seemed unaware of it, hahaha.

Caesar (he can barely hear himself over the buzzing): WHAT'S THE BIG IDEA, YOU SHOWBOATING CUNT?

It wld've made an ideal caption had it been given the opportunity.

Prating Pontifax: I've always considered myself a spiritual communist, actually. Christ was a fish out of water. But that doesn't mean we shld throw the water out!

The Princess Legerdemain, in lizardskin camisole made distressingly translucent: Christ was out of wine. But G.O.D. can always be counted on to find the very smallest fish to fry.

Carbonara Inverso, reclined in a deckchair on the far

poolside, took a polaroid of Legerdemain's tits & wafted it about, trying to get the image to stick. The water beneath her was littered with rejects (nothing if not the perfectionist).

Pontifax: Hell, my dear, is a fishwife.

Legerdemain: Pimped in a fishy manger.

Sobremango, sprawled in an inflatable armchair, cast one Magellanic eye at the wider environs. With it he spied Bandera in a pair of bespangled speedos mesmerising the radical fringe under a spindly palmtree. Bandera quivered, blustered, perorated, sounding exactly like a pamphlet by Bandera.

That! mewled Legerdemain, following the poet's gaze, is the summa cum laude. I rest my case.

Hahahaha! cried a voice from on high. It was Dona Cinquenta, pissed as a parrot, swaying in a hammock between the branches of an overarching fig.

Pontifax: Fly, darling! Spread yr beautiful fleshy wings & fly! I, the most divine Juno, queen of the gods, doth command it!

And so she did.

THE GREAT WHITE BAT

Orange still streaked the western horizon, Mars ascendant, moon not yet risen, when from the ruined battlement above the orchard behind the House of Hands came a strangulated shriek &, moments later, the spectral thing, sweeping over rooftops, ineffable & monstrous against the dying light. Albufarkas cld not've testified to what he'd seen, in the sense of a physical perception, but he was in no doubt whatsoever that he'd stood in the presence of an entity both transcendent & appallingly real. By rational deduction – Kingdom: Animalia. Phylum: Chordata. Class: Mammalia. Order: Chiroptera. Family: Vespertilionidae. Genus: Nyctalus. Species: N. lasiopterus. Congenitally deficient in pigment? Or, by irrational induction – raised from the dead? Albufarkas wld insist, whatever the mechanics of resurrection, a ghost by itself is nothing, if not empyrical, an insurrection of the senses. To behold aghast this blighted entity, w/ one's own eyes, therefore, being the sole criterion, in which its certain existence cld be judged, or not, by means etc. A rent in spacetime haunting Europe. A transmogrified Minerva, paragon of inwit, hunting through twilights of idolatry its proxyself. Photons estrangely entangled. Tragicosmic television. How I wonder do the stars see thee? Twinkletwinkle plastic bat. And I, too, entangled by turn, a glitch of spectral video to those other, immaterial witchers of ancient Anizar, re-gazing at this precise patch of vaguely resemblant yet distinctly nonidentical sky, creatures of parallax, owlish? I to them, a mock of paraselene? A glint in His Master's great white arse, most rare aurora, Look! Look! There upon the Milky Way! like some replayed flibberty ejaculate condemned to conjugate the aeons, over & over, eternity by the stairs, hahaha, till right set wrong, this foul unpublished crime, a farce's murder! Pure ham! Cld it've been otherwise? Or only the same unwise? Returnal spam! Yet what if this aberrant apparition were more than merely a misprismed mimesis? Harebrained hypnotism? Harbinger of demented doom? Guilty conscience shrieking in the night? Apologise! Apologise! Or Oedipus will come to pluck out yr eyes! (For what crime?) (Of witnessing, my pretty little fuckwit.) (Whispers Narcissus, slipping between yr thighs.) Like a mental ignis fatuous, floating out from the hole in Albufarkas' proverbial third eye, into the world, hungry for gratuitous morsels of. *Invasion of the Body Snatchers*? Albufarkas can't tell one from another. (Not for the first time.) (The Great White Bat by all accounts being a "phenomenon," like the stray black cat that creeps down yr stairs in the middle of the night & empties the garbage all over the kitchen tiles just to get a lick of a sardine can, widely reported in the month of July.) (An owl, a bat, a cat?) (Once more in the Land of Thrice.) Is he sleeping or awake? Oh & since when was such a distinction – hark! did you hear that? Rat w/ wings! (He's going bats, quaternally!) (Going, going, going, gone.) Swoops from one shadow to the next. Braille-eared. Echolocutor. (Knows when y're listening to it.) Brainwave oscilloscope. Pale wing. Weaving the monastic belfries in Visigoth silhouette. The chesspiece chimneyspires. The microwave minarets. Lunate battlements of the Cormanesque castello, faintly wisped. And if he, Albufarkas, were to grow leathery gauntlets in his sleep, a cape of skin, wake in the image of man-upstrung? Flapflap, a jester in thy sky, amidst starry space w/ cut-out tongue, mouth stopped-full of black humour, too much wit in one head to be healthy, the talking tumour. Condemned ever after to be that thing. Not by own choice needless to say. Up there watching till cockcrow. Motto: vigilantibus! Two-headed bat on a field sable. Vampyr & antivampyr. Siamesed. I entangled, soul of souls. Blood-percipient. The pulsing night. Hung from a hook. As one-by-one the stars sped westward away & there was nothing left in the sky but a vague anaemic sense of abandonment. A great white bat resplendent.

TOURO! TOURO! TOURO!

Heat bulls in off the plain. Olé! Its horns turn in the last dank crevices of dawn, gashing & cauterising in one stroke. Sobremango prosed it thus in his head, a deft line, he self-congratulated, stroking his matador's cape. The beast wld invariably end on its knees, just as it was paid to do. Sobremango pondered the monstrous flanks. His breath stank of sour grapes. His erection had failed. You were meant to pierce the beast w/ yr sword in that secret place. Behind the Corrida at 6:00a.m., when all the respectable citizenry of Anizar were still groping their pillows in befuddled sleep. Sobremango grunted, wiped a copious dew of sweat from his eyes. The beast yawned. A carriage drawn by a bowlegged nag lurched up the cemetery road. What was the use carrying on? For the sake of literature the poet buttoned his flies & put in the boot. If nothing else, a man had to uphold his dignity. The beast dragged up its pants, spat, hand out for emolument. It cost more, failing to impress a natural order. Sobremango let the sundry notes flutter onto the dirt. Without a doubt the beast's hand cld've crushed his spine, had the thought ever occurred. Their entire transaction was pure theatre, he knew. The beast slouched contentedly off to its corral. Already the sun was unbearable. The gypsy-trap went clattering past the cemetery gates. And in no time at all, Sobremango was hunting for another drink.

João Sobremango's critics agree unanimously when pointing out the clearly defined stages in his poetic evolution. The first stage began in the 1990s w/ *Poemas para nada* (1992) and *Calçamanías* (1995). In these first books, the word acts out its deictic function *par excellence*. While the poet's first productions are defined by a certain linguistic ecstasy, the second stage gives rise to a sensation of the lugubrious, grotesque & deformed, as in *The Millenarian's Fosse* (2000). The third stage consists of *Perversión de los días* (2012) & *Enculada* (2014), through which a rich vein of "philosophical scatology" runs. The ostensible lyricism of these last poems transforms them into a homage to the Baixo Alentejo. According to critic Lázaro Limpa, "The eclogue-like atmosphere, the distempered language, the irreligious tone & patina of linguistic decadence, have turned Sobremango's latest offerings into authorial excreta of the most delectable assortment."

The people's poet regaled the habitués of the Charred Mongrel w/ his curriculum vitae. It was an aggrandised asshole-in-the-wall in the lee of the Castle. He quoted Kafka. He quoted Quixote. He quoted himself. Songs were sung. Wine flowed. A pair of snotgobbling cops slouching past on the earlybird beat. Protecting the insomniacs from their lesser selves. Sobremango saluted & the snotgobblers saluted back. He was a personage, Sobremango, ever so slightly immodest, hinted in undertones to the matron behind the bar. She gave a conspiratorial wink & lined up another carafe of the house's finest vinaigre. Sobremango sloshed out a glass. Scrutinised the bouquet.

Pure velvet!

Swilled some between incontinent lips. Clacked tongue. Sucked his dentures.

Like the down on a demoiselle's deltoid!

Without further ceremony he chugged the rest.

Ah! The infinite poem!

Ah! The empty glass!

And emptier wallet!

Sobremango climbed unsteadily on the bar, arms outstretched:

Amigos! We're like characters in a bawdybook intentionally left blank.

The stout matron swatted at his ankles w/ a wet dishcloth:

Speak for yrself, champ, you were stuffed to the gills before you even came in.

I am (hic!) the great Panto Mentor! The (hic!) Pun Tormentor! The (hic-hic!) Pen Tomographer!

Yr pin's popped, it's time you pushed-on, Pierrot.

Poo-hoo, the postman hasn't even passed the parcels yet.

It's a red-letter day.

That calls for another glass, comrade!

Sobremango's performance had begun pulling a crowd. Regulars gave ground to the early morning cognoscenti. They plied the people's poet w/ all the fulsomeness at their command. In short order Sobremango obliged, regaling all & sundry w/ the unedited volumes of his *Œuvres complètes*. From the corner of his eye, he spotted the mayor & his cronies sidle onto barstools to take in the show, flourished some well-oiled pith, the mixed metaphors flowing freely as from a bottomless carafe.

Anizar! Radiant hole of the universe! You spasm against capitalism's grasp like the rectum of Karl Marx! You lubricate w/ the divine accommodation of an infinite muscle able & willing to encompass the sun!

And on & on & on & on.

Cld any audience have savoured more the embarrassment of riches, the cornucopia of sentimentality, the sheer superabundance of cliché? With each successive recitation, a surfeit of the most hackneyed literary devices: stream of consciousness, disappearance of the omniscient author, unreliable narrators, fragmentation of plot, extreme self-reflexiveness, intertextual games, collage, pastiche, sexually audacious themes, the incorporation of cinematic techniques, blahblahblah. Everybody who set foot in the Charred Mongrel that day deserved an honorary PhD. On it went till long after nightfall, when, to the incredulity of an audience already resigned to a Promethean fate, Sobremango, midsentence & mouth ajar, tipped incongruously sideways in his chair &, w/ sudden ungainly momentum, jackknifed onto the floor, out cold.

I survey w/ an eye cruelly formed, the last riot of a dying sun…

A smattering of stupefied silence coming undone as the remaining clientele beat an opportune retreat out the door. The matron flipped on the radio. The mayor took a selfie w/ the prostrate poet & had it relayed post-haste to the *Anizar Gazette*. A CULTURAL TOUR DE FORCE! (debauched, w/ unconscionable predictability, by the morning edition typesetters into ACULTURAL TURD OF FARCE!). The eponymous mongrel, a steaming shagpile of impenetrable black, heaved down beside Sobremango's head & yawned. Man's best friend to literature's greatest servant. Such an occasion wld one day demand a plaque (HERE LAY, ON SUCH-&-SUCH A DATE, THE PEOPLE'S POET'S DOG HEAD).

SCHWEINHUNDERT DEGREES

So hot in the day yr eyeballs sweat, so cold at night yr tits freeze to the sheets!

Legerdemain lay on a pile of spilled mattresses in her "ghostroom" watching fog roil across the window leaving a faint glimmer of slime. A menagerie of white seasnails, white unicorns, white elephants, white rabbits & white rabbitholes. Take one step out there & you cld be lost forever. She let out a sigh meant to signify all the vagaries of metaphysical distress. Pontifax, splayed naked upon a faux Berber rug, in utter disregard of meteorology, scratched indolently at his flea-infested hide w/ an antique monkey-paw. Coughed. Prodded his liver. Stretched into a yawn. Physique as comely as a French bulldog.

Legerdemain: God why can't anything be as simple as it used to be any more?

Pontifax: If destiny dictated that humxnity were to do anything the easy way, we'd still be back sucking down bananas in the treetops. Why the hell else wld G.O.D. in His wisdom have invented the industrial revolution & computers & a cashless economy, if not to get His houris hand-delivered by flying robot? I really don't know what I've been doing wrong all these years. But I can tell you this much, no houris.

Legerdemain: Won't I do?

Pontifax: The only time you were hand-delivered, the word "robot" hadn't yet been invented.

Legerdemain: Says the spring chicken to the snow princess.

Pontifax: Shld we subject ourselves to the laws of idiots?

Legerdemain: I, for one, am subject to nothing. Speak for yrself, Ponty.

Pontifax: So y've come to specialise in exceptionalism?

Legerdemain: I've always seen myself as something of a generalist, actually.

Pontifax: And they say I'm overcomplicated!

Legerdemain: I am thinking of writing my memoires. *Confessions of a Predatory Cygnephile*, in honour of the Leda not recorded in myth.

Pontifax: Ah, already I feel trapped inside something interminable, like Proust.

Legerdemain: Sadly no pleasure is interminable, even mine, & y're free to leave whenever you can manage it.

Pontifax: I've been turned into a sow.

Legerdemain: Better save yr bacon then, senhora, before I ride you to market.

Pontifax: Hahaha.

Legerdemain: Hahahahaha.

Pontifax: Well, the very least you can say for *yrself* is that the rest of yr life is still ahead of you.

Legerdemain: And all of history behind me.

Pontifax: Between a rock & a hard place, then.

Legerdemain: My dear, you grossly overestimate *yrself*.

Pontifax: One shld have a cause to believe in.

Legerdemain: Or at least one to fear.

Pontifax: I fear we are like two people at cross purposes.

Legerdemain: Better than being two dead ducks at cross purposes.

Pontifax: Or two dolts w/ a cross to bear.

Legerdemain: Or two bores dead for a ducket.

Pontifax: Or two tweedles twiddling their thumbs.

Legerdemain: Or two tonguetied travesties in thumbstalls.

Pontifax: You know how this is going to end, don't you?

Legerdemain: Pre-emptively.

Pontifax: I've always been of the opinion that one shld get in the last word as soon as the opportunity presents.

Legerdemain: Ninety percent of any conversation is just testing the water.

Pontifax: Probing their defences.

Legerdemain: Feeling for a soft spot.

Pontifax: Setting the opposition up for a knockdown.

Legerdemain: Feinting & jabbing.

Pontifax: Leading them into a false sense of security.

Legerdemain: Letting them think they've got the upper hand.

Pontifax: Blinding them to their own vulnerabilities.

Legerdemain: Pulling the wool over their eyes.

Pontifax: Slipping them a Mickey Finn.

Legerdemain: Leading them a merry dance.

Pontifax: Up the garden path...

Legerdemain: ...& down the spout.

Pontifax: Like itsybitsy spider.

Legerdemain: On Miss Muffet's tuffet.

Pontifax: Not to put too fine a point on it.

Legerdemain: But under what conditions?

Pontifax: Stand well clear, is what I say.

Legerdemain: Timber!

Pontifax: As here I fall, so shall I lie.

Legerdemain: Having fallen so far was the intention all along.

Pontifax: As to the truth of the matter...

Legerdemain: ...let it sleep w/ the dogs.

Pontifax: On yr backs my pretty little fuckwits!

Legerdemain: Knock off their blocks my piratical fearwigs!

Pontifax: Insects!

Legerdemain: Aristocrats!

Pontifax: Aristotle!

Legerdemain: Axolotl!

Pontifax: What was the fucking point evolving just to come to this?

Legerdemain: Self-improvement, my dear, is a neverending journey.

Pontifax: I'd rather die a damp squib.

Legerdemain: They'll never let you get out if it that easily.

⚡PERIGO DE MORTE⚡

All evidence pointed to rain the morning the ancient widow two doors up from the House of Hands passed away. In her sleep, apparently. By the time Albufarkas' quizzical head cld be seen protruding over his balcony railing to stickybeak at the mise-en-scène below, the sun was mopping up the puddles, a couple of workmen were concreting potholes & a cop, stationed at the widow's door, was cracking jokes w/ a nurse swamped in hazmat coveralls. They'd been carting the widow back&forth to Nossa Senhora da Graça hospice for months laying bets on how long it'd be before the old bird finally kicked the bucket. It was a jovial scene for a Friday. They'd have the body bagged, the house hoovered & the paperwork paperclipped before lunch. It was a good deal all-round, the next of kin cld swing on down to picturesque Anizar for a dirty weekend of divide-&-plunder, before potting their conveniently forgotten matriarch on Monday morning. Barely a day of gainful employ lost. Albufarkas wondered how long wld be considered decent before festive FOR SALE signs festooned his neighbour's façade.

As the morning progressed, the old folk from all along the street cld be observed huddling superstitiously on the fringes, whispering to one another. Their eyes flashed. Albufarkas, inveterate voyeur, heard the widow's name echo among them. Isabel. Well, m'belle Isabel, the bells have tolled for thee.

FEAST OF CORPUS CHRISTI

It began, as was to be expected, in confusion. But was it history repeating or just one highly attenuated simulation of it, built around an imaginary event like neural scaffolding? *Because there's actually no body. It isn't that the word "body" is a metaphor: there never was a body. We have again been invited to consume such absence, to savour it, the divine non-presence of the saviour. The logos on the tongue, in which it speaks, speaking in tongues. Eenie meenie Ikey Mo. Given a sufficient timescale the Christ algorithm produces causal loops from sheer randomness, a crucifixion from a fractal curve. The non-body is a temple, a house of tongues. Yahweh. Babel. Ululata-lulu-la.* Imam Koan yawned. Another incomprehensible missive from that schlump, Albufarkas. Vey is mir! Always the goyish savages stuffing ideas in some dumb prostak's kopf. But why did the one semiliterate slob among them have to choose *him*, that is to say *me*, to persecute w/ the retelling of it? As if, like that imbecile frog, whatsisname, who said *everything in the world exists to end up in a book?* Well what sense did *that* make when the world *was* a book & the book *was* without end? It pains my kishka. I, Imam Bey Koan of the true Kohanim, who once went ten rounds of the board w/ Bobby Myseh before the flag dropped on Washington Sq. Knoweth thus whereof I speak. Listen, the only Jésus ever worth a dime was a short-order cook on 6th Ave., tossing hash for his sins w/ toast & three eggs sunny-side-up. So much for the Promised Land of brave & free (*everybody* who stands in line pays!). You think those WASPs, slaves to the hegemony of their own kitsch, were ever about to admit the Son of their God was a Puerto Rican? Well I had a home once too inside my dear dead matka's moneymaker, which just goes to show the limitations of nostalgia, aint it? Where do childers come from? The future, you idiots. Like the day I & I fianchettoed the aforesaid Bobby Myseh, hahaha, kicked the spasky prostak's bony arse. Bishop takes queen from behind the arras. And didn't the kid end up shitting himself right there at the table in sight of God & every other bum in the park. What a stink! I mean, you think *he* didn't dream at nights his mama was cherry? Every mensch his personal messiah, inshallah! Of course there're gonna be exceptions to the rule. Take ol' Gypsy Moe, pretended to skip the whole Oediprole routine, son of Pharaoh my arse, I mean who'd ever be able to live *that* down, why he never got so much as to plant his stubby little toes in the motherland, am I right? Setting an example to the tribes. I mean, what the hell d'you reckon the old beard was doing up a mountain forty days & nights in the middle of the biggest sandpit in the outer suburbs? You know how many words-a-minute that is? Ah, le mot juste! People aren't capable of appreciating craft any more. Like a quality crucifixion. Nowadays they'd be okay w/ a cheap bit of CGI. And all that *angel rolling back the tombstone* jive! Like that's the first thing cops are gonna investigate whenever a stiff gets nicked in the middle of Paschal. Put out an APB on angel-in-possession-of-three-day-old-stiff, potentially armed & dangerous. Meanwhile a bunch of horny undergrads are honing their fillet-knives in a Beth Israel anatomy theatre. Not kosher you say? Well no-one said anything about *eating* the guy, did they? Gotta make you wonder, though, about them tricky Christologists getting hip to dialectics, always talkin in reverse. Here, try a drop of this claret, dear boy. Fancy some crackers w/ that? Always that finger-of-blame gonna come pointing in the face of some unsuspecting alterboy-in-distress just happen to be standin on the white side of the tracks. Interrogator: So, erm, this feast yer talkin about's just *metaphorical* & not to say y'all a pack of *de-ranged cannibals?* No man, he aint even *dead,* he's sittin at the right hand of The Man, took his own body w/

him (coz it's a unique model, one of a kind), dig? Listen, son, falsifyin yer own death's a crime in this here backwater! Now I cld tell you about places where they claim to keep a morsel of the divine umbilicus preserved in a jar, but that'd be beside the point. The point my friends is Albufarkas. Perhaps *he's* the messiah, have you stopped to consider that?

84

GIVE UNTO CAESAR

There were, after all, countless many who refused to believe their salacious pseudo-Caesarian Salazarini was truly dead. A one-man walking spectacle of himself, hahaha. Ruler w/ an iron wad. The millimetres of his power exploded into a landscape of metrical flaccidity, syncopations, counterpoints. Carnal inner-ear of the city state's antipode. The dictator was bound to be swallowed up in it eventually. And so it was, splashed in black&white across the front page of the *Anizar Gazette*. SALACIOUS SALAZARINICIDE! There was a funeral notice on page three, the lying in state, the whatever-they-callled-it when a man of substance departed the body under unnatural circumstances. Ashes to ashpits & dust to dustbins. Caesar Augustus , ave imperator, gloria in excelsis terra, blahblahblah!

Legerdemain read aloud w/ a mighty dose of schadenfreude, if only to compensate for the sheer agony of existence. Her customary migraine hadn't begun until the morning-after-the-night-before was already well underway, meaning its onset found her marooned in the company of the libertine librarian, Epimedia Blavatsky, Die Dame mit der Peitsche, like a bad alibi. It was, she mused, like having a drunk fruitbat hanging around yr neck & naming it "Balls," as if it were a partytrick y'd left the party to pursue a lifelong relationship w/ only to wake up in the tackiest kind of zero-budget vampire flick involving rubber teeth & ketchup & bat vomit all down the front of yr prize décolleté.

Besides, the librarian had been a most unspectacular lay. All on account of that gelded grandee, Salazarini. The deplorable cunt was convinced she'd driven him to it, suicide no less, cold shouldered the poor bub into a watery grave, w/ that homemade batwoman get-up & plastic ridingcrop, boohoo. Which rapidly became unbearable till a bottle of postcoital cachaça put paid to all that. Homicide wld have appalled her less. Wld, in fact, have been vastly more satisfactory. But cld Epimedia be counted upon to do it? In some desperate quarter of Legerdemain's unconscious brain, feasibility studies were fired off among interested parties, but no consensus arrived at, before the curtains descended on the dream of precipitant action.

Only to part again on the cold light of midday, groping a fistful of aspirin down her throat, though not nearly enough to blunt the rising banshee-pitch inside her head. Like being chained to a peasant orchestra. And then the daily paper the cat dragged in w/ Salazarini's idiotic mug all over it. And a little while later Epimedia screaming out the front door.

NIGHT ORCHESTRA

Fog smothered the whole town. Wisps & vapours. Uneasy spirits. It was as much as Albufarkas cld do to see the Roman Walls from the top of his stair. Hulking ghouls in musty cerements. Mist spiralled, heaved, crashed w/ a silent ominous force. He was Ahab at his wheel, the House of Hands his ship. The bridge swayed. Any moment now they (he & it) might be driven onto the clashing rocks, looming silhouettes of craggy battlements. And if this bow shld split? No god at these latitudes.

A wet dew lay upon Albufarkas' flesh. Flesh like crabmeat. Under its brittle shell, naked self & its antiself.

Awake wretch!

In a sudden cold gust the words lost all vehemence, sucked back into their hollow lung. Echo & gasp. (Mustn't forget to breathe! Siphon down into the diaphragm this foul sub-Atlantic stench. All those drowned aeons regurgitated over vast Alentejo tidal flats. If he were to falter now. Down into the hell-mouth, belching its fumes.)

We are pathways! he protested to the elements, that were they able to listen wldn't have.

Albufarkas drove his forehead against the wind. A battering ram against, etc...

Let loose yr harpoons!

...as a great wall of white washed over & swallowed him whole. (Gregory Peck eat yr heart out.) Tumbling, arms outflung upon the foredeck, flat on back, cruxiformed. A grey film settling upon the eyes. No, not dead, not yet. The antipodal duality of resting beneath yr own two feet. He's found an entirely other climate down there, a stillpoint, a radiating heat, man of clay on the oven tiles. Pale tendrils entwine the stars. The retreating hiss of the great sea.

Albufarkas lay counting the constellations. A cicada chirped in his ear. Had Plato invented a philosophical instrument for representing the music of the spheres, wld he have called it a Glaukonspiel? Listen! Do you hear the great axis grinding away? Working its millstone? A spider tiptoed across Albufarkas' vision. Hoist on the rigging. Branches swayed. He had much he wished to explain to them. A man w/ a rusty thumb. Lubricate w/ óleo de nim. Tight fit: me, alterself & noman. Aye aye, chilblain! The spider abseiled down for closer inspection. Eight eyes to one, no contest. A closed mouth admits no flies. Fer cryin out loud, drag yrself off the tiles man! Time to mizzen himself to the mast. What good was temptation without the will to mistake a manatee for Maid Marion? But even a spider cld see he was all bluff. Back down into his manhole he scuttled, rolling off his back onto calloused hands & bony knees. Ark! Noo! Nude! Noodles! Frack! Frantic! Frangipanies! Christ on a kebab! Was this the meaning of redemption? On all-fours, backside to the wind, baldpate pointing east. There'd be other occasions, other orientations, to enlarge upon at a less inauspicious time. Roundaboutly.

Descend he did, by a corkscrew stair, the turning gyre of one returning from mystic heights as to a kitchen sink, for the sake of a cup of over-brewed tea. Greater men's destinies had dallied upon less. The beaches of Gallipoli. Ah yes, remember them well, old cock! No slaughter complete without the savour of Ceylon washing about yr dentures. Plus a dash of cardamom, to be sure. To lack cardamom wld be a cardinal sin, surely. A colonial sinecure let slip, sluiced in saltwater, upon the Turk's delight at fiery fusillades along the whole length of an indeed very steep cliff, up which no gravity-defying of excrements wld ever be shovelled, even by headstanding antipodeans, ho-dee-ho. In whose honour Albufarkas doused liberally the brackish concoction from a carton of prehistoric UHT. Sipslurped. Ah! What bliss. His equilibrium, to speak metaphorically, restored as the tannins hit his gut & tarred his intestine. Tanis feline god of Ol' Egypt. A black cat creeping along the wall upsetting the plant-pots sending loose rooftiles plunging guillotine-like down onto cobbles that only moments before some vagrant trod lucky to be all in one piece till the shadow-of crosses a corner up ahead & seven hairwrenching years a rancid karma clotting in yr gullet. Never know when fate goes whistling past the back of yr head, eh? Hear today, deaf as a post the next. Luck of the draw.

Albufarkas poured off a second cup, a third in due course. A great man for the tea, was what they said, the players of xádrez on the café terrace, opposite the Museo, pondering their n^{th} combinations, sipping time-to-time from glasses of milchkaffee, custard-&-millefeuille filigreeing shirtfronts, fossils-in-waiting. Albufarkas w/ a pot always of Earl Grey, closest approximation, English opening, pawn to queen's-bishop-four, indirect insinuation. And will no-one rid me of this meddlesome priest? Gladly. Perched streetside, in hot umbrella shade, taxidrivers feet up on steering wheels, a couple of undertakers black suits ties uncorking their siesta, the hour between the wolf & the yid, hahaha, sweat streaking under chessmen fedoras, a couple of labourers under an awning deadeyed watching to see if anything'll happen. Cut back to:

Gulped his tea.

Old leatherguts.

Keeps you well preserved, at least.

Albupharaonic.

Keeps you up at night, pissing rivers, at least.

Albupsssssssss!

As they say in the protoclassics, drink sufficient quantity of the stuff &... By Gulliver! Tsunami at dawn! There go the stables! The horses! The haybails! There go the bums in the park! The unemployed poets! The players of xádrez! There go the little chessmen afloat upon the steaming tide, umbrella tilted to jib, working the tiller, out across the great urinal & onward to the wide western sea, salt in their beards, law of diminishing returns at their backs. All things being probable. Few things being provable. A marginal number being profitable. And where did he, Captain Albuforce, stand on the issue? Exploitation of the masses for exploitation's sake? HOW FAR Y'RE TAKEN FOR A RIDE'S JUST A MEASURE OF HOW BIG YR IMAGINATION IS, motto for the day. For the working week. For the life given joyously over to relentless grind, w/ its trinkets & baubles traded for the Promised Land. Well, on the matter of cosmic realestate our dear Albufark cld by now count himself an old hand, getting a little long in the tooth, even, mark of extinction, hahahoho. And what if, tomorrow or in five-minute's-time, a stranger waving dollars were to knock upon the door? It's a done deal sunshine, all the powers that be are in agreement, signature mere formality, consider this a purely symbolic downpayment, can't take it w/ you's what they say, ain't it? House of One-Hand-Washes-The-Other. So much for the mango tree, eh, dear Albufun? Have to plant yrself some other environ, preferably under a parkinglot, technically wldn't have to pay the meter till you leave, hihihihi. Make automobiles imaginary, 's what I say. Solve half the planet's woes right there. Magic carpets, teatrays, tipped tables. No wheels good, four wheels baaad. Who'd've thought the humxn mind wld end at the combustion engine! Like discovering gravity, before which anything was possible. Does anyone even remember who said the sky's the limit? Limit of what? The refractive index?

Albufarkas sliced off a hunk of loaf & spatulaed on the butter. Milhafre dos Açores, *com um toque de sal.* Stuffed it down to sop up the bilge, the ballast, the intestinal scoria. Worked both ways apparently. *Last Tango in Paris.* And wld fair Albufarkas facedown on the floorboards find anything of substance to fret about if, at that precise moment, Marlon Brando were to slither from his brainfog &, while maintaining an unbroken stream of monologue, perform scenes of impromptu sodomy? Chère Albufarque in well of loneliness. How wld he write that? Breakfast at midnight, buggered by Brando. Though customarily, for that particular repast, he erred towards yoghurt & banana. See if the Freudians can wrap their dirty little skullcaps around that. Pot of stewed Arabica, also, for its laxative effect. It's important to obtain the correct nutritions at the appropriate diurnals. To promote, among other things, healthy neurological function. Stimulating the gluteal cortex. Palpating the hippocampus. Etc.

Ah the labyrinths of solitude! Of passion! Of indigestion!

You shld quit while y're ahead, sneered Albufarctus' alterego out of the pit of his teacup, a buttery gob pendulating $T=2\pi\sqrt{L/g}$ from lower lip.

Cld this be what the philosophers called Dasein?

Ah well, the betrayal of humxnity.

Look, d'you really think we belong in the same neck of the woods let alone the same genepool?

I'm alive, aren't I?

That's hardly a good enough reason to think y'll get away w/ it.

Christ this does get tedious all the time, one time after another, all the times bleeding into each other, it's a frigging bloodbath, it's the mother of all menstruations, haven't you had enough spewing yr sickness into my ear?

Albufarkas chewed his fattened crust.

How to make the most of the day ahead, that was the thing. Before the sun got over the parapets & went to work baking the chlorophyll into the brickwork. Rusty bathtub w/ mad proliferation of leafmatter browned by spidermites from Mars hahaha. Erotic zucchini flower, overriperuptured cherry tomatoes blistering the teracotta, dissident ozones cackling down from the ironosphere, to dissolve in oceanic mists or fragment or objects & creatures left on shore. Meaning, carnage among the plantpots. First fogged then fried. Après le déluge & all that. And he, humble Albufark, on his Noah nobby, saving every sad sack that happened to set down roots in whatever roofcrack availed itself. Wherefore to be so compelled?

Murrrrrr-nau!

There, one of the cats mewling down the chimney. Oh my daughters! But Albufarkas' saviour complex needed its sleep. He set his alterego for 7 o'clock. The sound of snoring came thick & fast. Time enough for ants hauling away fallen breadcrumbs. Time enough.

SCREAMING IN ELEVATORS

Anizar Gazette: What, in yr view, is the role of the intellectual in society today?

Sobremango: We live in police systems. There are a lot of more or less developed police systems. We can ask ourselves what the ingredients of the criminal thought are. I'd like to approach them w/ reference to poetry, for which I have a fairly precise method. There is a certain crime against the police-state that always, can only, assume the form of a poetic act.

Anizar Gazette: Is it possible to live outside representation & discourse?

Sobremango: Firstly, death is the most common way of life. I'm not referring only to social, spiritual or intellectual death. I mean that the majority of humxnity lives *as if it were already dead*. But they are unable to represent this fact to themselves, because death itself, in its pure reality, is unpresentable. So, in a sense, yes.

Anizar Gazette: Does intelligence mean to comprehend before acting?

Sobremango: Comprehension is action 24 times a second.

Anizar Gazette: Is literature comprehension or action?

Sobremango: Today literature can't even speak to itself, it doesn't exist.

Anizar Gazette: When you write, do you already know what y're going to say in advance?

Sobremango: Sometimes I have a very clear premonition of impending disaster, like a film in which the protagonist does the very opposite of any rational person & this creates a sequence of events that move fatalistically towards an end visible to everyone else from the very beginning. This is a quite specific genre in which uncertainty plays almost no part. Its utter irrationalism makes it, ironically, paradoxically, the very image of a rationalist artform. But insofar as I determine in advance that I am going to write, *what* I write remains shrouded in the profoundest mysteries of spontaneity. And this is the only kind of writing that makes any sense to me.

Anizar Gazette: Does the diegetic universe annex the real or the reverse?

Sobremango: I've heard that there are mathematicians who believe that the universe is nothing but a hologram projected from a higher dimension. I'm interested in what the narrative implications of such an idea cld be.

Anizar Gazette: Are those who embrace paradox engaging or simply amusing?

Sobremango: Paradox no longer exists, politics destroyed it.

Anizar Gazette: When does the difference between writing & thinking cease to exist?

Sobremango: In the end, if you want to make a distinction you have to go back to mathematics. To establish a proof, it's necessary to *prove*. You don't demonstrate an idea, the idea itself must be demonstrative.

Anizar Gazette: What does literature make possible that life doesn't?

Sobremango: Nothing.

Anizar Gazette: In writing, is it the subject or the object that acts?

Sobremango: What reflects, the image or the mirror? Writing is the inscription of the world, in both senses simultaneously.

Anizar Gazette: The only way literature can be deciphered is as a failure to transcend itself?

Sobremango: Literature dreams itself as another, as an art without rules & whose only rule is that the existing rules are false or misapplied. This dream of freedom is the basis of its dogma, which is its reason for being.

Anizar Gazette: What does it mean to be alienated & aware

of our alienation at the same time?

Sobremango: It means that existence demands a capacity for irony.

Anizar Gazette: Is this the situation of literature?

Sobremango: The irony of literature is its literariness.

Anizar Gazette: Or does literature only function to the extent that it remains, in fact, unaware – that its claim to awareness is just the mark of a more profound alienation?

Sobremango: It's true that literature represents to a large degree a latent fascism which even its irony cannot hide.

Anizar Gazette: Is this why a literature of emancipation will always be impossible?

Sobremango: To say that emancipation is impossible, it's not that simple. It wld perhaps be better to say something else or see things somewhat differently. In the end, what I find interesting is that the only point really in common between literature & everyday life is this question.

Anizar Gazette: Can we only love for the wrong reasons, then?

Sobremango: If love has any meaning at all it is as alienation's counterpart & constant companion, as Narcissus to his reflection.

Anizar Gazette: What does literature become when it ceases being aware of itself & simply acts?

Sobremango: Psychosis.

Anizar Gazette: If all writing is literature why doesn't all writing have the social function of literature?

Sobremango: The name of the name isn't the same as the name.

Anizar Gazette: Do you agree that meaning is like resurrection?

Sobremango: To be *like* resurrection wld be the walking dead. In that sense, yes.

Anizar Gazette: Is it necessary for literature to be as ambivalent about humxnity as humxnity is about it?

Sobremango: The question is, does humxnity truly exist? It isn't so much whether or not literature has anything to say about this existence, or nonexistence, but to what extent it produces it. Perhaps humxnity's existence depends entirely on the extent to which literature expresses the opposite.

Anizar Gazette: Can poetry save the world? Or can it even save itself?

Sobremango: As everyone knows, there's a tacit alliance between the corporate mafia & the police state against the quote-unquote terrorism of radicals, militants, avantgardists, etc. At least since Plato, a certain idea of poetry has been annexed to this war on terror, which is to say the suppression of insurrectionary tendencies before they invade the general cultural field. Not insurrection for its own sake, but tendencies directed at the edifice of *meaning*, which is to say *of the status quo*, which is to say *of the world order*. Poetry can only save itself to the extent that it's conserved *in opposition* to this world. And it can only save the world to the extent that it's possible to *save* an enemy.

BUT I DIGRESS

The animal is walking up rua Alferes Malheiro on its hind legs it's opening a door w/ its. The animal is waking up on rua Alferes Malheiro on its back it is opening its eyes without. The animal is walling itself up on rua Alferes Malheiro on its hands & knees it's opening its mouth to. The animal is willing itself to breathe on rua Alferes Malheiro on its side it's opening a void into which it can at last, etc.

THE IDES OF MARCH

The coroner, disgruntled at having his Saturday-night game spoiled, slouched over to the bodybag, tossed a butt on the ground, spat, took one look at the victim & declared autoasphyxiation in pursuit of risible intercourse. Still a chance of catching extra time. Penalty shootout. Never the same watching the replay, knowing it was all past history, like the shmuck w/ the stocking over his head & the piano wire cinched around his privates. Who did things like that? Families were known to picnic in the vicinity. You want kids splashing about w/ a stiff in the water? Keep it in the closet, was the coroner's sage advice to the self-abusing demimonde. Locked. And swallow the key.

Of extenuating evidence recovered at the crimescene, not the scantest trace. A couple of frogmen paddled about in a rubber dingy, making a show of dredging among the reeds, going through the motions. A bored cop prodded the corpse while the coroner took a call. The stocking was torn around the mouth in a ragged grin & a wad of paper jammed between rows of yellowed dentistry.

Well curiosity can get the better of anyone & whadyaknow the cop reaches down & extracts a dozen sodden square inches scribbled over in lamentably delible blue ink from the stiff's buccal cavity. Spreads it out under the moonlight, getting smudged verbiage all over his pink mitts, only to find himself, unbeknownst, fingering the ostentatiously literal titlepage of a certain malefactor's misplaced MS, a bruise of purplish blotted prose & the halfdissolved yet potentially incriminating cognomen, all caps, A-L-B-U-F-A (for such it was):

What kind of *prevert* writes drivel like this?

Now precisely what possessed this officer of law&disorder to wipe his mucky paws on said artefact & lob it, wadded into an approximate sphere of diminutive radius, over his shoulder & into the marsh, there to drift past the dredgers into the allconsuming dark, may never be revealed. Ho-hum. Still plenty more ungurgitated spurious prose propping apart John Doe's molars, enough to fill an evidence bag for the eggheads in forensics to fervidly misattribute. (Well there goes yr shot at literary fame, old son.) *Needless to say, this illconsidered action won't've been inconsequential for what's yet to come.

Right then a goon from the *Anizar Gazette* came swashbuckling through the tinder armed w/ a telephoto lens the length of his forearm. (Flash!)

Say cheese for the citizens, coroner. (Flash!) Who's the gimp w/ the foolscap stuffed down his throat? (Flash!)

Coroner to cop: Zip the goddamn bag, why doncha?

Goon to coroner: Gonna be someone in town w/ a piano don't tune right, eh? Wonder who that'll be.

Coroner to goon: What note d'you reckon we shld be listening for?

Goon to coroner: Middle-G, hahaha.

Cop: What the fuck's that supposed to mean?

Goon to cop: Don't sweat it, flatfoot. Any clues?

Cop to goon: Yeah, some *prevert* skulking about w/ a camera & a bunch of compromising pictures of the deceased, that wldn't be you by any fucking chance wld it?

Goon to coroner: What I love about this job is just how predictable the repartee is.

Coroner to goon: Missed yr vocation, you shld've been an actor instead.

Goon to coroner: Have you seen that theatre crowd? I mean, talk about déjà vu.

Coroner to goon: You wldn't happen to know the score wld you?

Goon to coroner: C'mon, when was the last time we won anything?

Coroner to goon: Hope burns eternal.

Goon to coroner: Yeah, well there's a few others I wldn't mind seeing burn eternal, but what're the odds?

Cop & a couple of medics heave the bodybag over to the back of an ambulance & shove it inside.

Coroner to goon: I shudder to think who that's gonna turn out to be.

Goon to coroner: No-one you recognise, then?

Coroner to goon: What do I look like, a flaming *prevert*?

Goon to coroner: Takes all types.

Coroner to goon: Wldn't you know.

Goon to coroner: Aw, I'm just doing my job best I can, Frank, like if they'd let me into medical school maybe I'd be doing yrs.

Coroner to goon: Now who's kidding who?

Goon to coroner: I've got rent to pay & a cat to feed.

Coroner to goon: That's yr problem right there, cats drive you nuts, it's scientifically proven, if you aren't nuts in the first place, I mean who voluntarily lets a creature like that into the privacy of their own home?

Goon to coroner: I don't suppose you get too many stiffs wash up like that around here?

Coroner to goon: We get some. They just don't all get reported that way.

Goon to coroner: Not enough piano wire to go around?

Coroner to goon: I have it on good authority the stuff can be obtained at any self-respecting hardware store. You cld try running w/ that.

Goon to coroner: C'mon, Frank, what's yr theory?

Coroner to goon: Officially I don't have one.

Goon to coroner: Unofficially?

Coroner to goon: Well, what we've got is a male, caucasian, middleaged, balding, potbellied, splindlylegged, mouth full of rotten teeth. Not exactly yr average Adonis, so either he paid for it or the other party has a fetish for ugly little men. By the look of things, it happened pretty recently. Fingernails were filthy but hands hadn't seen a day's work. Politician most likely, hahaha. No evidence he struggled, so voluntary, unless someone made it look that way. My guess is he croaked during the foreplay &

the other party didn't want the headlines, so shipped the corpse. Probably up at the weir. Floated down w/ the current & some local out walking their mutt spotted it. Amateur job.

Goon to coroner: Unless it was meant to be found.

Coroner to goon: Here we go.

Goon to coroner: I mean, even in the movies...

Coroner to goon: Screw the movies.

Goon to coroner: Who've the fuzz got on it, apart from flatfoot over there?

Coroner to goon: Meyer Gordo. *Detective* Meyer Gordo.

Goon to coroner: Where's *he* hiding then?

Coroner to goon: Consulting the horoscopes, I wldn't wonder.

Goon to coroner: Did you look to see if the stiff was circumcised?

Coroner to goon: I've got enough trouble as it is.

Goon to coroner: Trouble's yr business, Frank.

Coroner to goon: So it is. So it is.

Goon to coroner: Are those clowns in the dingy there to catch guppies or what?

Coroner to goon: Why don't you ask them.

Goon to coroner: No evidence, then?

Coroner to goon: Y're the tabloids, fella, isn't that yr speciality?

Goon to coroner: Hahaha.

Coroner to goon: Hahaha.

Goon to coroner: Hahaha

Coroner to goon: You know, if I were you, I'd try the phonebook.

Goon to coroner: Madam Blavatsky's Bondage Parlour, *par example*?

Coroner to goon: Now y're cooking.

Goon to coroner: I'll let you know how it goes.

Coroner to goon: Save it for Gordo. He'll love you for it.

Goon to coroner: No thanks. Like I said, I've got a cat to provide for.

Coroner to goon: I think there's an expression for that.

Goon to coroner: You might be right.

WAS TIME RUNNING BACKWARDS, OR JUST IN THE OTHER DIRECTION?

Amerika is like a vampyr that goes around sticking pictures of itself on every mirror it can find, while Ruzzia is the imp slithering along behind it that adds a shit moustache, opined Sobremango in a voice not quite amniotically soothing but near enough.

A pair of bats swished past Carbonara Inverso's head. The tsk-tsk of a mosquito-zapper in the background. Pontifax snoring in his paddlepool. Carbonara Inverso gazed up at the moon hanging in the sky above Juno's Temple – like an eye disguised in a painted diorama, she thought, that looks back at you & sets the whole world tilting at angles *très* Caligarique. Geometries of unwellness.

God forbid they shld ever actually wage war upon each other, the poet drawled on. That'd defeat the entire purpose of their existing in the first place.

Well, we're all proxies now, dear, thought Carbonara Inverso without saying it aloud. She was afraid of interrupting the Great Man's flow. Like disturbing someone mid-piss.

Sobremango, for as long as he remained suitably pensive, cld tranquilise a wild rhinoceros. Her own voice, in contrast, evoked comparison to a wheezing deathbed confession. On account of a recent bout of influenza. Even her vocabulary had suffered, as if the language itself had got infected or rather was the infection itself passing from mouth to ear to lung like an intubation-event unfolding in timelapse. Even when she managed to get the words out, their sense seemed to trail along behind them at an overly discrete distance. She barely knew what she was saying before she'd forgotten the details already.

The fact is, said Sobremango, that modern Ruzzia was born of the same mystic ecstasy that produced the touch-tone telephone & the hamburger bun.

But, wondered Carbonara Inverso, was it a proxy war that'd somehow reached across the breadth of Europe & laid its hand so awfully upon their happy world? "La morte de Salazarini!" Lowering the shutters, bolting the doors from the panic-terrors flying freely around the ancient streets, hell-bats in the mass-hysterical belfry. Caesar's praetorian guard had thrown up roadblocks all around the city. There were rumours of a coup d'état, vengeance killings, a general rounding-up of perverts, intellectuals & anyone w/ a political opinion. Under the circumstances, even Juno's Temple cldn't be considered inviolate.

Let them smash the doors down! Pontifax had proclaimed, as Pontifax would, before medicating himself into a stupor. The goddess will avenge!

And so, Sobremango, not to be outdone, intoned, will poetry!

Be that as it may, nothing very adequately explained how the until-quite-recently omnipresent Palhaça Arsénio Salazarini had met w/ such an insalubrious end, under a weir at Sangue do Rei – by a lonely stretch of the Old Kingdom Road – in the direction of the archaeology digs.

MANYFACETED AS A MAHARAJA'S GALLSTONE

And then of course there was the sad story of Johann Haslinger, musician & sculptor from Linz who, in 1900, according to legend walked on his hands for 55 days, 10 hours-a-day, from Vienna to the Exposition Universelle in Paris, when strictly speaking he was strapped to an amputee's two-wheel cart that he "paddled," barehanded, over variable roadways for 1,435km (pre the International Convention relating to Automobile Traffic). The distinction, minor as it may appear to those unappreciative of its gravity, is crucial. One is a form of humxn locomotion w/ body in a vertically inverted orientation w/ its full weight bearing upon the hands. The other is a mode of horizontal propulsion, modernist in spirit, presaging the coming technical revolution of the century. The Reichsautobahn only began construction in September 1933, under the direction of Hitler's chief engineer Fritz Todt, initially a 14-mile expressway between Frankfurt & Darmstadt, which opened on 19 May, 1935. It may, of course, be mere coincidence that Hitler attended school in Linz.

Sobremango had theories about a great many things, but about the Death of Salazarini he had only forebodings. Besides, Epimedia had been a nervous wreck for weeks, even a blindman cld see what was going on. Had Caesar himself crawled all the way from Rome over broken glass & used syringes, he'd've fared no better & deserved no less. A woman scorned! Ah! A plot to savour! Thesis colliding w/ antithesis!

From which no synthesis issues, merely a tragicomic effluent of disillusion. It was necessary to crawl up into the very bowels of it just to stay above the tideline. Otherwise you drowned. Fucker fucking fucked. Indeed, Sobremango's entire philosophy might be summed up as the somewhat inebriated passage from -er to -ed by way of -ing. Entire doctoral theses ought to've been written about it.

Salazarini hadn't needed to crawl all the way from Rome, or Vienna, or even across the Praça da República. The length of a Steinway wld've been more than enough. For example, the Steinway in Madam Blavatsky aka Senhora Epimedia's second-storey boudoir on Dos Infantes. What Sobremango *really* wanted to know, was how she'd gotten the fat little slob's body down the stairs & all the way out to Sangue do Rei without leaving a trace.

PLAGUE OF FLYING ANTS

On every available surface they crawled, punchdrunk, bulbous black, winged, monstrous, to what vile purpose? First the rain, percolating through cracked & shivered stucco, overspilling the leaf-littered drains, flooding the foundations, causing last vestiges of whitewash to malt from lichen-riddled walls. Then the ants. Their perilous ascent from underworld into the pure mimetic light. A countless abomination of them. Emerging as from the very air. Air thick, viscous, decadent. The kind of air you cld strain through a sieve. Or a dishcloth. Or a sodden manuscript.

Well don't expect any sympathy from me, Antifarkas yawned.

The aggrieved author stared forlorn into his empty satchel. Staring thus hadn't caused his truant manuscript to rematerialise. He mentally prodded himself in the retracing of steps, the whole tortuous itinerary of twists & turns, for convenience here abbreviated to bed, café-bar, biblioteca, bistro, park bench, bath, & now, ensconced on the balcony of 10 rua Alferes Malheiro, Bandera. Not literally Bandera, but a literal attribution nonetheless, on the very front page of the afternoon edition of the *Anizar Gazette*. Where, just moments before, Albufarkas had, w/ toes contentedly curled inside his babouches & a pot of tea resting warmly in his crotch, blundered upon the telltale turns of phrase & most idiosyncratic typographical disfigurations of which he himself cld only have been the instigator. Most astonishing! And more astonishing yet, for this plagiarised purple prose was purported not to be some errant work of untold genius but an incriminating excerpt from a cryptic anarchist manifesto for the premeditated overthrow of the state (author sought on charges of sedition & assassination of a certain unnamed public official, prime suspect Bandera, believed to've gone into hiding in the general vicinity, citizens of Anizar warned not to approach, potentially armed & dangerous, anyone w/ information to contact the Guarda Nacional Republicana posthaste etc.).

Perched on the balcony railing, Antifarkas smirked.

Nevertheless, it does present a rather juicy dilemma, eh what, old bean?

Like the seven plagues of Egypt, y'd suppose, wrapped up in newsprint.

But in that particular literary universe, who wld play the man-of-destiny writ large & who the patsy? Who the serif & who the serf?

FLY ON THE WALL

The swivel-chair turned on well-lubricated bearings as Meyer Gordo plucked a fly out of the musty air w/ an audible twang, then came to rest soundlessly at a 90-degree orientation to the detective's oversized mahogony desk. To a casual observer, the chair's composure in time of crisis, as w/ Gordo's itself, was palpably Zen-like. Not so the gluttonous lipslobbering that accompanied the hapless fly's ingestion.

The goon from the *Anizar Gazette*, however, knew it was all an act. The dead flies invariably wound up in the top drawer of Gordo's desk – pure sleight of hand made it appear he ate them. Suspects, superiors & the generally unwary were left ill at ease. He said the protein from flies' brains was what gave him the highest case-rate in the whole Baixo Alentejo. Who was going to argue w/ that? The goon proposed an exclusive. Gordo reached into his drawer & pulled out a fistful of flies, letting them sift back through fingers each an inch-thick:

You want I shld order out for knish?

That's quite some stiff yr boys bagged over by Sangue do Rei.

Ach, these bags they are unfortunate, but also necessary. Perversion behind closed doors is just everyday life, but out in the open it's a public menace. We, of all people, must set a positive example.

Gordo punctuated this last sentence by sliding his desk-drawer shut w/ a muffled thud. As if to say, Out of sight, out if mind. But cld it possibly be?

Anyone we know?

You saw yrself, victim barely had a face, barely even humxn.

Whatever it was, or whoever it was, will take more than our friend the coroner's dark arts to deduce. Let us agree, simply, that it was a gratuitous act. Just how gratuitous is to be seen.

It was true that the corpse had looked like an offering to savage gods. To be honest, it looked like a great many things probably best left unmentioned, but the one thing it didn't look like was the Mayor of Anizar. Which was kinda funny, as far as the goon cld figure, since twenty bucks said that's exactly who it was.

After an hour in Meyer Gordo's waitingroom, flipping through the City Hall's bespoke full-colour glossy brochure – wherein a certain P.A. Salazarini's grinning mug leered out at the defenceless reader from somewhere on every page – the goon had no doubts whatsoever. Caesar Salazarini & the stiff at Sangue do Rei where one another's spit. How Gordo cld sit there w/ a straight face pretending otherwise was an absolute mystery. Or maybe it was just the case that, stripped of any vestige of power, the sonofabitch in the bodybag was just a nonentity like everyone else. If only it were possible to say the bastard wldn't be missed.

The goon figured he had till morning to get the story, before every last idiot in town had put the numbers together. He chuckled. Headlines paraded before his inner eye:

ET TU BRUTE? SEX MURDER SUICIDE SLAYING! CAESAR SALAZARINI GETS IT IN THE NECK. CASE OF MISTAKEN IDENTITY? PORNO POLI PERISHES PIANISSIMO! COPS PUZZLED OVER WHO PULLED THE PUPPETMASTER'S STRINGS. BLOODLUST OR CRIME PASSIONNEL? BOONDOCK BODYDUMP! MAYOR MAKES BIG SPLASH GOING OUT. Etc.

You cld work it every which way. It was a gift.

INDEX LIBRORUM PROHIBITORUM

Paper roses festooned the dressing table. Trophy locks of stolen hair. A panto parrot w/ ringbarked neck. Reams of filched manuscript. Fetishes strung around the mirror on antique magenta ribbon. Such untold secrets as Epimedia's boudoir might be caused to disgorge wld be like spiking the Xmas punch w/ emetic. A not unwelcome thought. Perhaps she shld. At least someone shld. The annual preening of stuffed shirts around the Nativity, chucking the infant deity under the chin before yawing off to the catering tables.

Epimedia dabbed a severe powderpuff at her cheekbones, sneered at the glass, pouted. Approximately 2000 years ago the god-king of the Israelites had raped a girl somewhere in Palestine & 33 years later came back to murder her child, told her it was in the best interests of all concerned. Epimedia's gaze settled upon the pages of manuscript as she thought this. Ah, to kill a man's bastard child. The wrongborn. Well, that Senhor Deus musta been quite some guy. But what was he to her, or anyone, in a town like Anizar, last layby on the road to the End-of-the-Earth, whose rune-riddled capstones conveyed more chronology, more credence, than any pseudo-Sumerian?

Such was the tangent of Epimedia's cogitations when the sound of shattering glass & toppling masonry brought to an unscheduled halt her transformation into the proverbial Madam Blavatsky, purveyor of unusual services, bewigged, corseted, spike-stilettoed. The cause was not long in coming. Boots pounded up the stairs, the door to Epimedia's boudoir unceremoniously kicked-in.

Epimedia spun around. Standing in the doorway, & in no way disguised by the red bandanna tied across his mug, was Pablo Bandera, putative revolutionary, resplendent in black knee-high Doc Martens & a pair of speedos, pointing some kind of blunderbuss.

DEATH TO THE FUCKING BORZHWAHZEEE! Bandera screamed, detonating a quantity of tiny lead pellets directly into Epimedia's astonished face.

VIDA LONGA À REVOLUÇÃO! shouted the comrades crowding up the stairs in Bandera's wake.

They promptly tore the room apart.

Bandera, kicking the martyrised librarian off her stool, raided the dressing table. Mascaras, pomades, khols. He grabbed hold of the stolen manuscript, immediately recognised the crabbed scrawl as belonging to none other than that freak Albufarkas, & stuffed it gleefully down the front of his speedos. Man & priapus straddled the expiring Epimedia & yowled a hideous warcry.

I'd finish you off, he winked down at her, but I like you better this way!

Epimedia spattered a bloody sigh over the remainder of her chin. If she attempted speech, it was lost in the ensuing convulsions. The poor dear really wasn't a very pleasant sight, but something about her eyes was rendered most expressive, as if a strange awakening, a kind of foreknowledge...

Bandera, after admiring his handiwork a moment longer, gave vent to another frightful yowl, then rousted the mob back out into the street, trailing their loot.

Now well may you ask how a selfsatisfied psychopath like Bandera cld be so improbably discerning of what had lain on Epimedia's dressingtable. Dank habitué of subterranean poetry readings? Albufarkian manqué? And what of Epimedia herself, a woman of inscrutable motive & obscure compulsion? Were we to rewind the clock, we might discover, only moments before, our hapless librarian & crypto-dominatrix, perusing those very pages, stained w/ an irregular pattern of brown rings, galão runes, eccentric & half-circles, bits of broken alphabet, a D perhaps, an O, a G, smudged into a single image legible only to a mind nourished by the fantastic. Had Epimedia Blavatsky intuited some divine presence, prompting her uncharacteristic fit of kleptomania? Was Albufarkas their Satanic Majesty's anointed messenger? Were these the secular scribblings of a hand guided by the profane unword?

And she, Epimedia, being – till Pablo Bandera's unscripted intervention – the sole custodian of this profound & most terrible insight. Terrible, terrible! Shld even the etherest whiff of it get out, Literature itself might swoon & plunge headlong into chaos! Sobremango no more! She cld hardly bear the thought of it. All these unrequiting, unrequited & oh so vulnerable creatures! But wasn't poetry love? The purest kind? Like the scent of isopropyl on a ridingcrop. A surgical swab. The blue flame of an acetylene torch. She, Epimedia, wld protect them all, each according to their unspoken, their unspeakable, neediness. For what good was a poet without a muse to carry the torch? And what good was a muse that didn't know it?

Thus it came to pass that – daily oppressed by shelves & shelves of dumb unresponsive books – the keeper of João Sobremango's reputation, the people's poet, found herself disturbingly aroused by the masochistic prosody of Albufarkas' pen. She had, in short, indiscreetly peered into his briefcase while the anaemic author was called by nature to a facility on the upstairs floor of the Biblioteca. She'd not known what she expected to find. It was like uprooting a man's dirtiest secret without even laying hands on him. Epimedia immediately knew exactly what course of action to follow & from that day on, whenever the oddity in the black fedora darkened the Reading Room, she found occasion to filch a random page of manuscript. At last count she had more than a hundred of them, piled neatly on her dressing table, the better to fondle them in her moments of enfilthed transformation. Their author's wrenching turns of phrase trespassed even upon her severest routines, invading a conscience driven by the inflicting of consensual punishment upon others, upon herself. That such a worm of a man cld elicit so complete a derangement of the senses!

But did Albufarkas not put two & two together after all this time? Let us conjure him: He searches & searches & searches for whole page-long passages he cld swear he wrote down. There are gaps in the flow of the work, but it's a work made of gaps. He can no longer be sure what was intention & what happenstance, what serendipity & what misadventure. Did the manuscript even exist? Had it ever? Was the whole thing a work of hallucination? Perhaps Albufarkas was afraid to know & so left the question hanging. Yet if we were to surmise that he'd hallucinated the writing of it, reason itself insisted he was just as likely to've hallucinated the losing of it.

IN VERBO VANITAS

If writing can be *summarised* at all, proffered Sobremango, this carries the same meaning as *summary execution.*

He gave a shrill laugh, solitary among the conclave of unamused officialdom. They had selected him for some kind of public honour, the point of which, he knew too well, was to award themselves the laurels of discernment by which authority flattered itself as the final arbiter of the beautiful & the good, amen.

So how shld the world speak about yr books? the goon from the *Anizar Gazette* said at the start of the Q&A, bored already.

Why shld I care?

Why shld anyone?

Because we're slaves, that's why, Sobremango wheeled his arms, in a manner that might be described, in those kinds of novels inclined to do such things, as *emphatic.*

Err, to Literature?

Emphatically fucking not! the people's poet crushed the arm of his chair for emphasis. Officials coughed nervously.

Right, glad we got that sorted. Any other piquant words of wisdom y'd care to divulge to our readers?

You mean you *have* readers?

Don't *you* have readers?

They're an endangered species, you never know, were you to look for them, if they'd still exist. Better not to. Like Schrödinger's cat. Only there's always the chance that, *if* you look, the cat will be *both* dead & alive, & leap out of the box to tear yr face off.

Zombie felines, eh?

Ever wondered what the afterlife wld be like, were such a horror ever caused to exist?

Haha, I always assumed *that's* what Literature wanted to be. The mouthpiece of posterity & all that. Voice of the great undead.

You might be onto something there. How about a drink?

Sobremango gesticulated at one of the lackeys hovering about the edges of the audience.

A bottle for the People's Poet, he chortled.

Bit early in the day for me, demurred the goon.

Rubbish, it's bad luck to be sober after midday. Death in the afternoon & all that.

Speaking of which, one last question...

Shoot.

Did you kill Salazarini?

CALLING ALL PORTUGEISTS!

A SPECTRE IS HAUNTING ANIZAR, THE SPECTRE OF SALAZARINI! Thus proclaimed the *Final Communiqué of the Antisalazarian Front, Anizar Faktion (AFAF)*. Beyond that, the revolutionaries' prose devolved into psychotic babble, a collage of Albufarkian gibberish, inspired by what, who cld tell? Chaos, one might suppose. Nihilism. Some category of anarchist Void. *The hour of enchained Prometheus is past! History belongs to the present! Let it burn! One man's tome is easily another man's tomb. Ah the good old days when a selfrespecting ape cld still sit around a campfire & chew cud! Let the beast merit the beast! The Salazaristas spread terror like lard on broken bread but can't stomach their just desserts! We've come to smell the cheese! Prepare thyselves! The reckoning is ripe!*

Picture him, Bandera the Bold chomping a cigar, w/ gluestick & scissors, at work upon his plagiarist masterpiece, seated on the terrace of Luiz da Rocha, n^{th} coffee at his elbow, a plate of demolished pastels spilling over onto the table wmong the dregs of an ashtray buffeted by the winds of change. Ever-industrious, the revolutionary who never sleeps, striving for the perfect performance. Meanwhile, upon the boarded-up storefront across the street, the phantom figurists of the AFAF had struck again, pasting an enormous caricature of Salazarini like some Brazilian despot w/ his arse on fire dancing through the gates of Hell, the Junta's new general HQ, hahaha. *GO RIMBAUD, DO THE WATUSI!*

The mood on the street was not quite as festive, though. Oh but why not? Had the mass of ungrateful humxnity not woken to a ringing of bells, gunshots & general jubilation?

Pablo Bandera glanced up from the abomination of cut&pasted Albufarkiana he was in the midst of manufacturing & beheld Florida, silhouetted against a barricade at the foot of the street, w/ a rifle slung over one shoulder, the shoulderstrap carving a line between luscious breasts. Orders were to shoot members of the Establishment on sight. Sinister shadows prowled along the ancient city walls. AFAF units roamed door-to-door. A tumbril passed by the café terrace w/ a dozen corpses slung over the sides. The driver saluted Bandera. Bandera sneered. Princess Legerdemain's corpulent mug ogled him upsidedown. *Au revoir, espèce de vache stupide!* The tumbril trundled on, jostling its sombre cargo, like some Frankenstein monster of a soon-to-be-extinct social class. And just then sunlight streamed through a break in the clouds, a merry omen. *Joy to the world! Death to all lords & masters!* Happy Easter indeed! A fine finale to that manyauthored cosmocomic conspiracy. A new scripture today is born, hip-hip-hooray!

Bandera's only major regret was that he hadn't strangled the bastard himself, but had to content himself w/ carrion. Yet who wld ever know? Once the revolution was complete, it was just a matter of pulling on the loose strings till the whole business of Salazarini's untimely demise was tied up in one great big messy knot he cld safely affix his moniker to, LIBERATOR OF ANIZAR! SLAYER OF PSEUDO-CAESAR! I, BANDERA OF THE BULGING BIKINI!

The sun struck his eye & stayed there, gleaming like a divine madness burning a hole in a piece of celluloid. Such is the bluff all melodramas are made of. As once upon a time, lying on the dead grass under a eucalypt tree, on the far edge of town, listening to the Great Cicada Monologue. Heat filtering down through the leaves. The heavy scent of coiled bark. The seed of an idea germinating among the fetid prions of Pablo Bandera's juvenile brain as he masturbated incompetently into his handmedown shorts.

But this reverie, too, must end. And as it did, a pastry van skidded up the street & came to a jaggering halt outside Luiz da Rocha's café, pastelaria e restaurante. The rear doors were flung open & out jumped an AFAF commando balancing a milkcrate full of broadcast equipment, immediately followed by another dragging a goon from the *Anizar Gazette*. The first commando set about busily extemporising w/ lengths of electrical cable & a microphone stand. The second thrust the goon at Bandera's table, saluted, spat over his shoulder.

Comandante!

Dog!

Bandera momentarily parked the gluestick, unchomped the cigar, eyeballed the startled goon, then thrust the pile of random manuscript pages at him.

Publish every last word of it or die!

What is it?

Don Quixote, whadya think?

The goon glanced at the coverpage:

Exclusive?

Get the fuck outa here!

Fastforward past the goon being hustled back into the van, etc. Bandera at his table, cleared now of its debris, microphone planted in front of him. A ripple of feedback through the civic PA system recedes in dopplereffect along the street. Bandera taps the mesh furtively. Gets the thumbs up. Assumes the demeanour of the Man of the Moment. A camera snaps.

CITIZENS OF ANIZAR! the PA boomed.

GREAT PLANISPHERE

Something kept blotting-out his sun.

The weather inside Albufarkas' head was grey, wet, cold, but mostly grey. Well what did he expect, the Hanging Gardens of Babbleon up there?

If he squinted hard enough through the dirty pane of glass above the stairs he cld almost make out his alterego grinning back down at him. Making a butterfly w/ its hands in silhouette, a cat's cradle, a cockscomb, the head of a wolf, a shape very much like someone flipping the bird. Why all the hostility old friend?

Atop a wobbly ladder, positioned on the stairhead, a length of nylon cord around his neck, Albufarkas waited w/ something approaching an air of resignation for the effects of the gas he'd left turned on at the stove to cause him to plunge or in any case totter into the eternal abyss, all things being relative.

Such was the cunning of a plan in which we might unkindly picture him having exulted before deliriously putting it into effect.

A sudden wave of peristalsis mars this image. The pseudo-stylite wobbles perilously atop his ladder. Gags. Turns a pair of pleading eyes heavenward. A strange wheezing sound emanates from his throat.

Eli, Eli, lama azavtani etc?

Hahaha the voice from on-high.

From somewhere, nowhere, a vague songlyric tresspasses upon the moment's solemnity. But it's only in his head. *I dance on vaseline...* It repeats w/ annoying insistance. Wld this be the last thought he'd ever have? But no, there's still time for a whole medley of them. *Slip-slidin' away... Don't bring me down... Peace love hang ten... Devil at the crossroads...*

The gas was meant to be odourless & colourless (though in Albufarkas' dreams it was always white, streaming into his mouth & nose like ectoplasm in old sepia spirit-medium photographs). In fact it tasted of lead, presaging the sleep of lead caskets.

Puke bejewels the front of Albufarkas' undertaker's suit. The stench of it comingling w/ the stench of butane & the antiseptic of recently mopped floors.

This wasn't how it was meant to end, but it was the end he got.

RECONQUISTA

"In this deep solitude & awful cell," like Cortisol's lament to Epinephrine, a veritable mapamundi of the punishments inflicted on sinners in hell, such was its aberrant poverty. Echoes of that pathologic carpentry, tortured beyond compare, of the former convent chapel, presently Museu Rainha D. Leonor, public viewings daily except Mondays. Bas relief vistas of medieval morbidity, retribution's alibi. An ABC of how to feed a six-century grievance. Christian martyrs flayed, quartered, seasoned, skewered, marinaded & broiled by salivating Saracens, hmm. And once again has history's egg come home to roost. Heralded by the soothsayings of the incommiserable, the disaffectless, the congenitally comediocre. *But why choose me?* "This House of Hands shall be thy mausoleo!" Oy vey! What a line! Such iambs! Such pantomeaters! So now the imbecile was raving about the End of the World. Give a narcissist a pair of binoculars & what do you get? E pur si muove! And all it is, is a case of flatulence, wiggling the little bellybutton. Imam Koan tossed the latest epistle of his erstwhile antagonist, Albufark, into the wastebasket reserved exclusively for that purpose, observing w/ distaste the burgeoning mass beginning to spill over the sides. The way that meshuga manuscrapt of his had turned up mangled *almost* beyond recognition (yet sadly not quite, eh?) on the front page of Anizar's obscurest backwater tabloid no less, posing as some mad militant's messianic manifusto (clipping appended herein). So now the schizoscribbler thinks he's Gaucho Marx, eh? Concocted a selfaggrandising homunculus Albufargonaut on a mission to steal the Golden Shower, hoho? The world must quake! The idiot's lost babblebook in the wrong mits unspeaks Creation's abracadab! So, it had come to that, gevalt! Newts & frogs! The dead re-arrise! The mirrors crack & their reflections run amok in the streets! The dog has its day! The collected works of Sobremango suffocate children in their sleep! I's, O's, U's on a homicidal rampage! Miscreant alephbats in the belfry! So much for universal literacy, teach a moron to type & this is what you got, reams of flagellant sanctimonious gobbledegreek. One day soon they'd have machines for that & humxnity cld go back to beating out its laments on forehead & rubicund behind, as of yore, in the mould of the Cosmic Immiserator, He who first made them in His rearwise image. Oh woe is Man who, discontent w/ his hindquartered house of horrors, must pound his poison pen like some Pied Piper zapping a guilttrip on the hoi polloi! The devil does indeed find work for idle hands. An opposable thumb up an apposite hole. Spoiler alert! Is this where evolution terminates? Like an uncut salami locked out of the Pearly Gates? Just another chump w/ a boybeard who can't get past the bouncers into the Big Blouse Club so takes it out on an Olivetti? I've got pains of my own, goddamn it! Why can't gazas just be gazas no more? It ain't like I got shares in the company, but some people is like having a whole crowd. I mean, just look at this socalled Albufarkaktus, watchya gonna do w/ a schmuck like that, pin a medjoul on the guy? I got half a mind to go down there & do it myself, 'shallah. House of bleeding Hands!? Y'd think he'd caused a mass murder, all the troubles he goes on, I have to read another word I'm gonna crap my wits. You wanna know what that famous newsclipping says? It says not a fucking thing, capische? Someone flushed it down the bog or something. Left it out like a piece of cake in the rain. Like a lilypad in a lake. Like a floater at a flood-barrier. Nothing but smudgy ol' blottopaper & slugtrails. Mailmensch musta got waylaid by a tsunami of epic proportions. Y'know, force majeure tampering w/ the evidence & all that. Me, I only believe what these here blinkers tell me. Ain't like the worldwide conspiracy circulating a printrun of the Protocols in invisible ink. What's that Albufug take me for, anyway, the

Father Confessor? Harriet Shaw Weaver? Max Brod? You reckon I oughta care about some 'maginary *Moby Dick*, washed up out of the blue, care of Correios, Telégrafos e Telefones, from a rando on the wrong side of the walls? Ever *been* to Anizar? Coz I ain't never even *heard* of rua Alferes Malheiro before this hazmat Hasid harried my Hannukah w/ his yuledung groanings, twelve menses to the day if it isn't the full solar anus. Oh the absence of solace! Ah the abscess of Sollers! Will no-one rid me of this unmitigated pud? *Prezado Sr Albufarkas, lamentamos informar...* All of which is perhaps merely the longwayround beatingaboutthebush manner of a man like Iman Koan staring a riddle square in the face, squinting a little more intently into his wastebasket as the pennies finally start to drop. Like the sonorous ping of a cashregister on a hard sell.

MEDO NA MADRUGADA

At long last a bleary-eyed sun rose through the fog to look upon the new day. Vive la révolution! The birds cheered. The trees waved. The chimneys sputtered. An empty bottle scuttled down rua Alferes Malheiro on the morning breeze. A stray mutt eased its bowels on the doorstep at number 10. Thus, Albufarkas, like the handle at the end of a toilet chain, from a higgledy-piggledy length of knotted rope, swung in the draught above the stairs in the House of Hands, for whoever, befitting the gravity of the situation, to stumble upon, were there anyone who might.

Beja
May 2022 - February 2023